The Kingfisher let out a high-pitched scream that would have done a woman justice. Then the tall, tan-complexioned man began to scramble toward the waiting car. He had to shove some of his bodyguards out of the way, but he managed to throw himself through the front door of the waiting Cadillac before the Ford reached them. Some of his gunmen, made out of better stuff, held their ground, pulling guns from under their coats. But the pistols were no match for the bursts from the submachine guns as the car roared past. All the bullets that struck the Cadillac bounced off because the car was bulletproof. But the men standing on the sidewalks weren't. They fell as if someone had cut them down with a mowing machine!

Holloway House Originals by Donald Goines

DOPEFIEND
WHORESON
BLACK GANGSTER
STREET PLAYERS
WHITE MAN'S JUSTICE,
   BLACK MAN'S GRIEF
BLACK GIRL LOST
CRIME PARTNERS
CRY REVENGE
DADDY COOL
DEATH LIST
ELDORADO RED
INNER CITY HOODLUM
KENYATTA'S ESCAPE
KENYATTA'S LAST HIT
NEVER DIE ALONE
SWAMP MAN

Special Preview of *Cry Revenge*—page 165

DEATH LIST

Donald Goines

An Original Holloway House Edition
HOLLOWAY HOUSE PUBLISHING COMPANY
LOS ANGELES, CALIFORNIA

DEATH LIST

Published by
HOLLOWAY HOUSE PUBLISHING COMPANY
8060 Melrose Avenue, Los Angeles, California, 90046

Cover by Jeffrey
POSED BY PROFESSIONAL MODELS
ALL RIGHTS RESERVED.

International Standard Book Number 0-87067-990-2
Printed in the United States of America

This Edition reprinted 2005

info@hollowayhousebooks.com

DEATH LIST

1

THE TWO DETECTIVES had been sitting in their office at the downtown police precinct since early morning, waiting for one phone call. When the telephone finally rang, both men leaped to their feet. The black officer beat his white partner to the phone. He winked at his friend, letting him know that this was the call they had been waiting for.

The tall, chisel-faced white man walked back to his old beat-up desk and sat down. Detective Ryan drummed his fingers on the top of the well-scarred desk as he waited impatiently for the call to come to an end.

Finally the tall black man hung up the phone.

"Well, what the hell are you going to do," he yelled over to his partner as Ryan jumped to his feet, "sit there on your dead ass all day?"

"Screw you, Benson, you cocksucker you," Ryan yelled back as both men moved hurriedly towards the door. "Did the informer give up all the information we need?"

Detective Edward Benson slowed down enough to show Ryan a piece of paper on which he had hurriedly written down an address. "We've got the bastard's address, just like he said he'd get."

The two men walked hurriedly down a short corridor that led into an outer office. The detectives threaded their way through the cluttered office, greeting the men and women over the hum of the old-fashioned air conditioner.

As the black and white detectives neared the outer door, two younger detectives sitting nearby came to their feet. Neither man appeared to be over twenty-five years old, while Benson and Ryan both had wrinkles under their eyes that were not there from lack of sleep. Both of the older detectives appeared to be in their late thirties or early forties. They were replicas of what the younger men would look like in ten years if they stayed on their jobs as crime fighters. The work would take its toll.

The two young white detectives ignored Benson and spoke to his partner. It was done more out of habit than to slight Benson deliberately. "We were told to wait for you, sir, that you might need backup men," the taller of the two said.

Ryan stopped and stared at the men. He hadn't missed the slur to his black partner. "I don't know," Ryan answered harshly. "It's up to my senior officer, Detective Benson." He nodded in the direction of the black officer.

The two young white detectives glanced down at the floor in embarrassment. Neither man wanted to come out and ask Benson directly if they could go along, but it would be a good point on their record if they could be in on the arrest of two murderers.

"What do you think, Ben?" Ryan asked his partner, breaking the silence.

Benson glanced coldly at the two younger officers. "It's up to you, Ryan, if you think you might need some help arresting the punks." He shrugged his shoulders, showing by his actions that he really didn't want the men along.

Ryan knew what the problem was. If the men had spoken to Benson when they first walked up, he would have taken them along gladly. But now he didn't want to be bothered with them. It was written all over his face. In the years Ryan had worked with him, he had come to find that the intelligent black man was extremely sensitive. At times, it seemed as if he was too sensitive. Ryan started to tell the young men to come along anyway but changed his mind. There was no sense in antagonizing the man he had to work with.

As Benson went out the door, Ryan turned to the two men sheepishly. "Well, I guess there won't be any need for your help after all. It shouldn't take four of us to bring in two punks."

It was apparent that the two men were disappointed. One of them started to say something but decided against it. Their brief exchange hadn't gone unnoticed by some of the other officers in the department. Most of them had been aware of what the men had been waiting for. As Ryan went out the door, leaving the men behind, the workers in the office glanced down, not wanting to catch the eyes of the rejected men.

Ryan caught up with his partner in the garage underneath the station. This was where they brought their prisoners. They took them out of the cars, still handcuffed, and led them to the three elevators that were located in the center of the garage. No matter where a policeman parked, he didn't have far to go to transport his prisoner. There were two uniformed policemen stationed in the garage at all times to help, if help was ever needed. The garage was also a good place for the policemen to kick the shit out of their prisoners, out of sight of any watching eyes. The garage detail never went against another officer, no matter how brutally policeman might treat a handcuffed prisoner.

"You could have brought those guys along, Ryan," Benson said, drumming his fingers impatiently on the steering wheel.

Ryan shook his head as Benson drove out of the garage. "Naw, Ben, it's like you said; what the hell do we need with help? It ain't but two punks that we're after."

Benson knew Ryan was lying, as well as he knew

he had been wrong in rejecting the help of the fellow officers. They were on their way to arrest Billy Good and his crime partner, Jackie Walker. Both men were believed to be professional killers. In such a case, there should be backup men on the job. If something should happen to Ryan because of Benson's anger, he would never get over it. But as he picked up the two-way radio and put in a call, giving the address they were headed for and requesting the support of a black-and-white car, Benson got a feeling of satisfaction. He knew that the two younger detectives would hear about it and know they had been rejected while two uniformed men had been called in to do what they had been refused the honor of doing.

Ryan only glanced straight ahead. He knew what his partner had done and realized that it was another blow to the pride of the younger officers. As it was, Benson wasn't the most liked officer in the homicide division. And after this got out, which it would, he would be liked even less.

"You think these guys will give us any trouble?" Ryan asked as they left the freeway at Clay Avenue and made a left turn.

Benson gave his standard shrug. "I haven't thought about it one way or the other. I could care less either way," he answered coldly.

Even as the policemen got off the freeway eight blocks from their destination, events were taking place that would change their lives.

Billy Good was parking the car in front of his and Jackie's apartment. Jackie kissed his girlfriend, Carol, one more time before getting out. They had just come from Kenyatta's farm, where they had been staying for the past week. Ever since making the hit on Kingfisher's dope pusher, Little David, they'd been out of town.

Billy, who had driven the whole way back from the farm, stretched his arms out, then caressed Joy's neck. The tall, black beauty riding next to him smiled contentedly. Joy had finally found a man she could really love. This short, husky, brown-skinned man wasn't what she'd dreamed her lover man would look like, but he'd proven he was more than adequate. She had no apprehensions when she was with him. It was a new and gratifying experience for her.

The men she'd had in the past had always depended on her, mostly for an income. Now she had a man who wasn't concerned with how much money she could make. He just wanted her for herself.

This was the first time Joy had ever been to the apartment that Billy shared with Jackie. She had just met Billy when Kenyatta brought him and Jackie out to the farm and had given a party in their honor. She smiled to herself smugly as she remembered that first night in Billy's arms. What a night it had been! They'd made love until dawn, and then she couldn't really sleep, afraid that when she awoke it would all have been a dream.

Carol and Jackie got out of the car first and waited on the pavement for Billy to come around the car and join them. They made a curious couple, him being over six foot five while she was only five foot.

Billy came around the car grinning. Neither of the two couples paid much attention to the well-dressed black men who got out of the black Cadillac down the street and hurried toward them. The first warning came when the men had gotten close and Jackie noticed one of them open up his suitcoat and take out what looked like a short iron pipe. Before he could react, he realized that it was a sawed-off shotgun.

He screamed out in panic. "Watch out, Billy, they got shotguns!"

The sound of his voice hadn't died out before the afternoon quiet was shattered by the sound of shotguns going off.

Joy had been admiring the new home she was going to move into when she was struck down. Half of her neck was blown off. Billy was spattered with the blood of his loved one. He screamed—a dying scream full of hate and frustration as he made a frantic move for his shoulder holster. Unknown strength kept him on his feet as the first shotgun shells hit him high in the chest. He fell back against the car, somehow managing to remove the gun from its place of concealment. But it was no use. He died with the weapon still in his hand.

Carol's screams shattered the stillness as she watched Jackie topple over, his tall frame crumbling as he kept falling until the hard pavement struck him in the face. Her screams were cut off abruptly as half her mouth and face were blown away. She was dead before she hit the cold ground.

Black faces peered out of the windows of the nearby buildings, but no one came to the rescue of the stricken couples. Blood ran freely down off the sidewalk into the gutter as the lifeless forms of four young black people lay in the filth and hopelessness of the hard-pressed neighborhood.

Down the street, the long black Cadillac moved away from the curb, filled with black men who made killing their business. Even as Detectives Benson and Ryan turned onto the street, the black car disappeared around the corner.

Benson slammed on his brakes next to the murder scene. The black-and-white backup car came from the opposite end of the street, having turned the same corner that the black Cadillac had.

Benson walked from one body to the next, examining the dead. When he reached Jackie's long body, he thought he heard a moan, but there was so much blood he believed it must be his imagination. He bent down and lifted up the bloody head, cradling Jackie in his arms as if he were a loved one.

"I think this one is still with us," he yelled out as Ryan came over.

Ryan flinched at the sight. He had seen many murders before, but whenever he came upon a shotgun killing, it was always horrible. This one was even worse than most. It was the first time he'd ever seen women shot down in such a vicious manner.

Ryan stood over his partner and called out to one of the uniformed officers who was running over with a gun in his hand. "Call for an ambulance," he ordered sharply, his voice cracking with emotion.

As Ryan glanced around at the other uniformed policeman, he saw the young black officer bent over by the car, throwing up his afternoon meal. The sight of the man puking almost made Ryan do the same thing.

Benson stood up. "He can change that call; we don't need an ambulance. What we need is a meat wagon." He walked away, unaware of the blood that was on his new blue suit.

2

THE PRIVATE OFFICE in the rear of Kenyatta's club was crowded with members. Ali had brought most of the main people in from the farm, and they were all trying to get in the rear office. The front of the club was full of the less important members of the organization. All of the talk floating around was about the killing of Billy and Joy, with little mention of Jackie and Carol. Joy and Billy were the better known of the four people. As they talked about the killings, the young people in the crowd couldn't really believe what had happened, or didn't want to.

The men spoke in loud voices about retaliation and the punishment that Kenyatta would dish out for the wrong done them. Even though Billy and Jackie hadn't been members, their women had been members. And Joy was related to Kenyatta's lady, Betty, so they knew something would be done.

Even as they whispered about it, Kenyatta paced up and down his office. "It has to be an act of retaliation, Ali," Kenyatta stated, stopping in front of the tall, baldheaded man. "No matter how I look at this shit, it comes up the same way. That motherfucking nigger Kingfisher is behind this crap. I'll bet my front seat in hell, man, that he put out the contract on Billy and them because of that pusher Little David gettin' hit."

Betty got up from the hardbacked wooden chair she had been sitting in at the rear of the office. The stately, beautiful woman walked up to her man and stopped. "But why, honey, why did they kill Joy? She didn't have anything to do with the killing of Little David. She wasn't even in the city at the time." Tears were running down her cheeks as she talked. "I can't get it out of my mind that it was my fault that Joy got killed."

"Hold on, baby," Kenyatta said softly, taking the girl's arm and drawing her near. He held her tight in his arms and stroked her hair tenderly. "Get them kind of thoughts out of your mind," he said as he gently led her toward his large chair behind the desk.

"It's true, though, Ken," she continued. "If I hadn't introduced her to Billy, it would never have happened. She wouldn't have been with him when he came back to town, so she wouldn't have gotten killed."

"Honey," Kenyatta whispered, "you can't think like that. The way them two fell in love with each other, it couldn't have went any other way. I mean, they would have met anyway. He stayed out on the farm after we left, so they would have come in contact with each other no matter what you did." Before she could speak, he continued. "Lookin' at it that-away, Betty, you can hold me responsible for their deaths, because if I hadn't given the party for them, none of this would have jumped off."

Betty stared up at the tall black man she loved. She gained strength from him, and at that moment she needed all the strength she could get. His words took her doubts and fears away.

She allowed him to sit her down in his chair. "When you talk, honey, it all makes sense, but when I get to thinkin' by myself, I keep seeing myself as the reason why she's dead."

"Well, don't think then," Kenyatta stated, ignoring the rest of the people in the office. He was tired of the crowd of people anyway, but he didn't want to dismiss them. He was going to need some of them as soon as some information came in, so he'd just have to put up with the crowd for a while.

"He's sure tellin' you right, momma," Ali said as he reached over on the desk and picked up one of Kenyatta's cigarettes. "The way them two carried on, it was just in the cards, that's all."

She glanced at the two men. They were so much alike, not just for the fact that they both were bald-headed, either. Both were tall black men, but whereas Kenyatta wore a beard and heavy mustache, Ali wore only a trimmed mustache. Ali was slightly taller than Kenyatta, too, though both men towered over six feet.

Kenyatta raised his hands for quiet, then spoke to the group in his office. "Fellows, you and the few ladies in here, I want you people to go upstairs or into the outer office until Ali and I can get something together. It's not that I ain't got faith in all you brothers and sisters, nor am I holding any secrets from you, but it's just that there's too many people in here now. We can't even hear ourselves think, so you go upstairs and have fun. I'll call the ones I want."

He waited until most of the people filed out the door. Betty started to leave, but Kenyatta waved her back down in her chair. "I'll tell you what you can do, Betty. Fix me and Ali a good cold drink, okay? Then come on back down."

She smiled at him as she got up to do as he requested.

Both men watched the tall, attractive black woman as she walked across the office floor. The thick, dark brown carpet smothered the sound of her high-heeled shoes, but nothing could disguise her large, beautiful black thighs, revealed to the eye by the miniskirt she wore. The tiny red skirt bounced up behind her with each step she took, causing Ali to give her a long admiring glance.

Both men remained silent until the door closed behind Betty. She was the last person to leave the office.

Ali let out a short whistle. "I got to admit she sure is a looker."

It seemed as if Kenyatta hadn't even heard his remark. The dark, handsome man walked to the rear of the office and stared out the window. He didn't bother to speak for a few minutes. "Ali, it's like I said. Ain't but one person responsible for this mess, and that's that nigger Kingfisher. I want him. I want him so bad I can taste it. That nigger is to blame for over half the dope that comes into the ghetto, Ali. Over half the fuckin' poison that finds its way into those dumb-ass addicts' veins."

Ali was used to his partner's ways, so he just remained silent and waited. "We," Kenyatta began softly, "were supposed to have knocked off that food-stamp place. That's what Billy came back to town for. I called him and told him to get his ass on back here if he wanted in on the stickup." He stopped as if deep in thought, then added, "Then them niggers shot him down. He must have just pulled up in front of their apartment when them motherfuckers cut them down."

There were actually tears in Kenyatta's eyes as he talked. Ali glanced away so that Kenyatta wouldn't realize that he had seen them. Ali knew that the killing of their friends had hit Kenyatta hard, but he hadn't figured it had hit him that hard. Actually, Ali could take it in stride. So a couple of gunmen and their broads had got knocked off. Those things happened when you played in the big leagues.

"I got a call, Ali," Kenyatta began, changing the subject, "from my white boy who's gettin' that list for us. He's got it. Now all we need is the cash I promised him for it."

That was something else Ali didn't agree with. Paying out all that money for a list of dope dealers just didn't make sense, even if they were the largest dealers in the city. The thought of ten thousand dollars going out for a piece of paper with names on it was just too much for Ali to understand. He wished at times that he was the leader. Then he'd run the organization differently. While it was a good idea preaching about knocking off the dope pushers, it would pay even better if they just made the pushers pay them protection. But Kenyatta wouldn't hear of anything like that. He was really sincere when he preached that shit about cleaning up the ghettos. If he wasn't, he wouldn't be wasting time killing police who came down on the brothers. Any time they got a report about any nigger-hating cop, Kenyatta started planning on sending the cop to hell.

"You still plannin' on payin' that 'wood all that money for that list, Kenyatta?"

"Uh huh, ain't nothin' changed. Why should it?" Kenyatta turned away from the window. "You ain't never been able to accept the idea of puttin' out all that bread for them names, have you?" He waited, then continued before Ali could answer. "I don't see why it's so hard for you to understand. Ali, the first time we knock off a pusher, we ought to be able to pick up more cash than I'm settin' out for the list. Man, all these mothers on the list are big, and do I mean big. They are the bastards that supply the dope

to the whole damn city, Ali. They ain't just neighborhood pushers, man. They're what you would call
international dope men. Just about every name on the
list will be a whitey, baby, so you can imagine the
kind of dough they should have around their pads."

For a minute the men's eyes met in a clash of wills.
Finally Ali had to glance down at the rug. There was
something fanatical in Kenyatta's eyes. It occurred to
him that the man was mad.

"Yeah, man, what you say sounds good," Ali
began, "but it might just be a little more difficult than
what you think. Them honkies have got guards all
over the fuckin' place. If they were easy to knock off,
somebody would have knocked them off before now."

"That's the goddamn problem with black men,"
Kenyatta stated coldly. "You big-ass bad brothers are
always ready to step in and knock off another black
man who's dealing, but when it comes to steppin' on
them peckerwoods' toes, you start shittin' in your
pants." Kenyatta walked over to Ali and looked
straight into his eyes. "I know damn near what you
think before you think it, Ali, and don't you ever forget it. I know you'd just love to be number one in
this outfit, but it wouldn't work. They wouldn't follow you for ten minutes. You think small and you'll
always be small." Kenyatta raised his voice. "If you
think I'm lying just look in the mirror. When I mentioned knockin' off them rich honkies, your face damn
near turned red, and that's one hell of a trick for a
black-ass nigger like you!"

For the second time in less than ten minutes Ali

found himself unable to look into Kenyatta's eyes. This time it was for a different reason. He stared down at the rug, ashamed of what he felt.

"It ain't like that at all, Kenyatta. I'm just lookin' at facts, man. Them honkies you're talkin' about ain't goin' be easy to reach. They don't even allow a black face out in them neighborhoods. That's why I say we don't stand a chance of knockin' them 'woods off."

"Niggers walk into banks and knock them off every motherfuckin' day, Ali, so why should it be too difficult for a black man to figure out a way to knock off some goddamn peckerwood just because he lives in a neighborhood that don't want any black people moving in? We got a few light-skinned black people in our organization, so when the time comes to stick up one of these places, we'll just use a few of them."

There was a slight knock on the door and Betty came in carrying their drinks on a tray. The men accepted them in silence.

She turned to leave, but Kenyatta stopped her. "Wait, honey, this may interest you," he stated, opening the desk drawer. "I wanted to knock the stamp place off on the first of the month, but since it's past, we'll just have to be happy with what we can get on the weekend take." He spread some blueprints out on the desk. "This is the layout of the joint. We'll send some people over to knock it off tomorrow."

Ali opened his mouth in surprise. This was the reason that people followed Kenyatta. When he made up his mind to do something, it was always done right.

3

THE ARMORED TRANSPORT driver cursed as he pulled up in front of the Food Stamp Collection Agency on Grand River Avenue. A tall black woman stood in front of a car with the hood up. She watched the driver closely as he pulled into a parking space two cars ahead of hers.

As soon as the truck was parked and the two guards got out, the tall woman slammed the hood of the car down. She seated herself in the car and watched the heavily armed guards as they entered the agency.

Inside the building a crowd of people seemed to be milling around, but as one's eyes became accustomed to the darkness, one realized that they were actually standing in separate lines. At the front of each line was a window with a teller behind it. There were bars over each window except at the bottom, where there was a large enough space for a man or woman to crawl through.

There was one security guard in the building and, when the two transport guards entered, he joined them.

There was a small wooden gate that led through to the other side of the windows where the women tellers worked. The guards joked with the black security guard as the trio went into the rear. The manager came out of his office and joined them.

They began at the cage farthest from the entrance door. The woman in the cage had to unlock her door from the inside to allow the men to enter. Inside it was like a small cabinet, fitted with shelves overlapping the small steel safe that contained the money. As each customer bought food stamps, the money was put in an envelope, sealed, and dropped into the safe, where it remained until the transport men picked it up twice a week.

As the manager stepped into the small cage, he removed a large key ring and inserted a key into the lock. Next, the guard stepped up and inserted his key. At this point the door swung open. Quickly the guard stuffed the money into the bag that his partner held. It didn't take long before the small safe was empty. They moved quickly to the next cage and followed the same procedure. Finally, they reached the last one.

By the time the last safe had been emptied, the

guards had filled three moneybags. Sweat stood out on the forehead of the guard with the key. He was a large, red-faced man with heavy jowls, ill-fitting clothes, and a huge pot belly.

"Goddamn this heat!" he cursed, not worrying about his profanity in front of the black female worker. The fat white manager grinned at him as they worked. They were two of a kind.

"I wish I could offer you a drink, knowing how it is," the manager said as they stepped back from the cage.

From out of nowhere a black man appeared in the section behind the cages. Before anyone could react to his appearance, another one appeared at his side. Both men wore long three-quarter-length summer coats. As the stunned group of guards stared at them, the men brushed back their coats and presented the sawed-off shotguns they held in their hands.

"What the goddamn hell are you guys trying to pull?" the manager yelled angrily.

There was fear in the manager's face, but overriding that fear was anger. He became a bright red as the blood rushed to his face.

"I won't stand still for it!" the manager yelled.

Instead of useless curse words, the heavyset transport guard went into action. He couldn't allow a stick-up. It would go on his record, a mark he didn't want, and one he wouldn't have. In twenty years as a guard he had never had any money taken from him. They had attempted to five years ago, three young black boys, but he and his partner had handled it. They had

killed two of the kids and wounded a third one. He
remembered the newspapers and all the publicity. For
a few days he had been a hero to the public and his
every word publicized.

Those very thoughts were running through his mind
when he made his foolish move. He fell to one side,
trying to make that fast draw he had practiced so
much. He never got his huge pistol out of the holster.

A third black man in the front of the group stepped
forward, raised the short-barreled shotgun an inch, and
pulled the trigger. The distance between them was less
than six feet. The shot nearly cut the guard in half. It
lifted him up off his feet and blew him back almost
the length of the room.

The second guard didn't fare any better. He made
his move at just about the same time his partner made
his. The second black man in the group shot him, and
the shot hit him in the face. Blood flew everywhere.
Where there had been a nose and eyes, there were
only gaping holes.

It should have been enough, but it wasn't. Whether
or not the black security guard acted out of fear or
the desire to be a hero would never be known. He
tried to clear leather with his pistol, but only managed
to join the other men on the floor. He clutched at his
stomach, trying to hold in his guts, which were pouring out of a huge hole in his stomach.

Whether or not he realized what was about to happen, the manager began to back up, pleading with each
step he took. "Take the money," he cried, "take it all,
but don't hurt me. See...." He raised his hands high

in the air. "I'm unarmed, you guys don't have nothing to fear from me. See" He stretched his arms even higher in the air.

As he begged, one of the black men in the rear ran past the other men towards the back of the building. He returned almost instantly. "It takes a key to open it," he yelled.

Screams of fear came from the crowd of predominantly black people in the front of the building. The black man standing in the front door holding his shotgun on them was beginning to have trouble from some of the fear-ridden women. "Stay back," he yelled loudly at them. The sounds of the shooting had just about driven them mad with fear. They pushed and shoved from the rear, until those in front were forced to move.

The gunman made up his mind at once. He didn't want to shoot any innocent people down, so he stepped aside. "Okay," he yelled out, "get the hell on." The stampede began. The women ran out the door, fighting each other in their haste to get away.

Some of them weren't so lucky. The old ones were knocked to the floor, then trampled by the frightened women behind them. Then someone shoved a terrified woman aside. The woman fell across the small counter-like shelf that kept the people away from the window. Others followed her, until there was a jammed up group inches away from the glass. Another gunshot went off, causing more bedlam, and this time the people nearest the glass couldn't push back hard enough. The ones in front went through the plate glass. Everyone was screaming in terror.

"We need the key that opens the back door," one of the holdup men yelled at the manager.

"Here, here it is," the frightened man yelled, snatching the ring loose from the small key chain. "Take it." He tossed it in their direction.

One of the men snatched up the keys and ran towards the door. The other bandit grabbed up the moneybags and ran after him. The third stickup man was undecided. He kept his gun on the manager until the fourth man reached him.

"Watch him for a second," he ordered, then ran to the rear of the building. The fourth bandit, who had been holding the crowd back from the front door, glanced down at the dead bodies lying on the floor.

"Shit!" he cursed, raising his weapon towards the manager.

The manager saw his own death in the man's cold black eyes. "Please," he begged, "please, I got a wife and k...."

The blast of the sawed-off shotgun was muffled by the cries of the women. The female tellers were crouching in their cages, screaming at the death around them.

Pain exploded from the manager's chest. He staggered from the force of the blow that struck him, but it didn't knock him off his feet. He could feel the pain even as the enveloping blackness prevented him from screaming out like the women. The blood-spattered wall held him up for a time, but the last remaining strength in his legs gave out and he crumpled up and slid to the floor.

As the murderer ran after his partners, the women inside the cages got up off the floor and fled. They were afraid the killers might come back.

Before the killer could reach the back door, he met the man who had ordered him to stay. "What did you do with the manager?" he asked quickly.

"I killed him," came the frank answer.

"Come on, then. We've got the back door opened," he stated, turning to lead the way. The man ran past him. Now there was only fear in the killers' hearts.

"Shake the lead out of your ass, Red," the man yelled back over his shoulder. "The fuckin' police will be all over this joint in a minute."

The man called Red didn't answer but just followed on the fleeing man's heels. When they reached the alley, the same car that had been stalled in front of the building was waiting.

Betty sat behind the steering wheel impatiently. She gunned the motor as the last of the men came out. They had hardly jumped in before she had the car in motion and was pulling away. The gravel in the alley flying from under the speeding car's wheels was the only sound heard inside the car as they made their getaway. The alley ended where another alley crossed. This was where Betty made her turn, taking a left.

There was clear driving down the long, empty alleyway. Betty slowed down slightly and drove at a more moderate pace.

As they passed a vacant garage, two boys came out and put four garbage cans across the alley. If there was any pursuit, the occupants of the following cars would have to get out and clear away the cans.

Betty smiled to herself as she watched them disappear in her mirror. Kenyatta thought of everything, she reflected as she drove even slower. That slight glimpse of the boys protecting their rear filled her with a confidence she hadn't had earlier. When she had first heard the gunshots going off inside the building, her first thought had been of fleeing. She had a hard time fighting down the desire to leave. They must have gotten busted inside. What other reason for all the shooting, she'd asked herself.

She came to the end of the alley and stopped. She glanced both ways before pulling out into the traffic. When they reached the next intersection, a police car came flying past, heading for Grand River Avenue. She waited for the speeding police car to cross in front of them.

"They must be on a code three," someone said from the backseat.

The sound of his voice breaking the silence also helped break the tension. The rest of the people in the car cracked up laughing.

"Goddamn, Eddie-Bee," Red said, holding his side. "Leave it up to you, man, and you'll make a funny on your way to hell."

The slim, brown-skinned man called Eddie-Bee smiled slightly. It made him feel good to make people laugh. It was one of the few things he really enjoyed in life, trying to be a comic.

Betty glanced over at Red sitting in the front seat next to her. "How did everything go?" she asked quietly. "You know, I heard all that damn shootin', so I'm sure as hell curious about it."

"I'll just bet your ass is," Red replied. "It's enough to make you curious." He stopped and twisted around in the car seat. "Our boy Zeke here started the ball to rolling," he began. "The fool-ass guard tried to go for his gun and Zeke sent him to see his maker."

The tall, slim, brown-skinned Negro sitting by the rear window moved nervously in his seat.

"Look here, brother," he began, speaking slowly. "I don't mind Betty knowing about it because she was up on the robbery with us. But after this, let's not do any mentioning of who shot who, okay?" he said seriously. "I know I ain't got nothing to worry about because all of us just about killed somebody back there, but I'm talking about when we get back to our club, let's not speak of who shot who."

"I'll go along with that," the short, plump man sitting between Eddie-Bee and Zeke stated. "There was too much bloodshed back there for us to talk about it. Them kind of things are best left untalked about."

"Don't worry, Charles," Red said casually. "Even though everybody in our club is cool, it is better not to talk about it. I'd even go as far as to say, don't even mention that you were on the job. Just being up on it is enough to get all day in prison."

Everybody in the car agreed with Red. Robert, the man who had run past Red so fast, gave a short laugh. "Shit, Red, as slow as you were moving, I'd have thought you kind of wanted to get cracked out. You know what they say, once a guy has spent as much

time in Jackson as you have, be becomes institution-
alized to such a degree that he really misses that way
of life."

Red laughed along with the rest of the people.
"Naw, baby, but havin' a foot race with you to see
who got out first wouldn't have been cool either. Just
like your running past me wasn't the coolest thing in
the world."

Robert started to argue, but Red cut him off.
"Kenyatta asked me to be in charge to a certain
degree, you know, so I felt it was my duty to see that
everything went off right. You ain't forgot, have you,
Robert, that I was on my way back in just to get you?"

For just a minute, Robert looked around sheepishly, then he regained his bravado. "Yeah, I know you
were, but you ain't forgot either that you ordered me
to stay there to the last and watch that fat-ass banker."

"Goddamn it," Charles cried out, "I meant to put a
slug or two into his fat ass. I hate a whitey who looks
like that bastard. I mean, you can actually tell he's a
flunky motherfucker on a black nigger's ass."

"Well, you don't have to worry about him no more.
That's one honky that won't be giving out any more
orders, unless it's in hell."

Betty turned onto a side street. "I hope you done
put them guns and money inside those shoppin' bags,"
she said as she pulled up beside a small compact car.
Inside was a woman who looked as if she was white.

The woman glanced up and down the street anx-
iously as Betty parked beside her. "Hi, Arlene," Betty
yelled as Red slipped out of the car and took the keys

from Arlene. He went around and opened up the trunk of her car and put the shopping bags inside. When he came back, he removed the trunk key from the ring before giving the keys back to the woman.

"Well, we'll be seeing you around, honey," Betty called out sweetly as she pulled away. She watched in the mirror as Arlene drove off. "Well, that takes care of that. Arlene is so light that, if the police should stop her, she won't have no trouble because they'll think she's a white girl and let her go."

"That's sure enough cool, but what's cooler yet," Zeke said from the back, "is that we ain't got that hot shit in the car with us no more."

"Amen," Robert said. "You can sure as hell say amen to that!"

When Betty stopped at another intersection a police car cruised past them slowly. The driver gave them the once-over, but seeing a woman driving must have thrown him off because he kept on going.

"I'll say amen, amen, loud and clear now," Red said, and they all laughed. They knew now that they could really relax. They were home clear. There was no more need to fear a bust. Everything had been taken care of.

4

INSIDE THE WELL-FURNISHED six-room apartment over the club were the people who had participated in the robbery. Kenyatta counted the money for the third time, then, after removing fifteen thousand dollars, made six small piles of money. He gave each person who had been involved in the robbery two thousand dollars. Nobody complained about the way he split it up.

"I for one," he said earnestly, "am damn glad that this shit is over with." Kenyatta glanced around at the smiling faces. "I guess just about everybody is happy, huh?"

Red tossed off a shot glass of whiskey before

speaking. They had been drinking and toasting each other since early that morning. "That ain't the half of it," he said, his voice sounding hard and cold. "I hope that finished it up for good. I hate robberies of any kind. That's why it's a shame Billy and Jackie ain't still around. They loved to knock over shit like that."

Kenyatta studied him closely before speaking. "You're one-hundred-percent correct about that, Red, 'cause that joint happened to be Billy's pet project. He'd been trying to talk me into knocking off that particular joint for damn near a year."

As he spoke, Kenyatta noticed Betty weaving through the living room, clutching a drink in her hand. He was momentarily surprised to see her stagger. He'd never before seen her drink enough to get loaded. She dropped into his lap, then rolled her beautiful eyes up at him. He noticed that they were bloodshot. He had a deep conviction that the past few weeks had put her under too much pressure. The only reason he'd sent her on the robbery was because he'd wanted her to do something that would take her mind off her Auntie Joy's death. There had been no way for him to foresee that the robbery would turn into a bloodbath.

He squeezed her small waist tightly. "Enjoying yourself, honey?" he inquired in what she termed his passionate bedroom voice.

Betty smiled up at him, her face lighting up and her pearly-white teeth gleaming. "You better damn well believe it. I didn't know Johnnie Walker Black could make you feel so good."

As Red stood up to go, he staggered. "I believe I'll

be gettin' on down the road," he said, picking up his money. "I got a date with an angel." He attempted to sing, but Kenyatta cut him off.

"Why don't you leave some of your cash here, Red? You don't need all that money in the streets with you at one time."

It seemed as if he might comply with Kenyatta's wishes as he stood there rocking back and forth, but the alcohol got the best of him. "Hey, baby boy, why you come down on me like that? I ain't no kid, you know. I can well take care of myself, brother."

This is the kind of shit that blows everything up in a man's face, Kenyatta thought coldly as he watched the man reel.

"I can take care of myself," Red repeated. Then he reached inside his shirt and came out with a pistol. "See, Ken, I ain't going in the goddamn street without some kind of help, brother. I wish a motherfucker would try and take something away from me." He waved the gun at the couple sitting in the chairs.

Kenyatta gritted his teeth. He knew exactly what he was going to have to do. There was no sense in wasting his time trying to talk the man out of his drunken plans. Kenyatta knew from past experience that, once Red started to drink, he was bullheaded and hard to reason with. Even trying to talk him out of the pistol would be a senseless effort.

Kenyatta hated what he was about to do. He tried to make his mind a blank and stifle any thoughts, because he knew he'd be arguing with himself. Who the hell was he to try to play God? The man had earned the money, so why not let him go out and spend it any way he wanted to? His answer to himself was that the man would probably end up shooting somebody. He would have to disarm him.

Kenyatta raised up out of the chair and set Betty down on her feet. "Come on, bro," he said, friendly like, "I'll walk you to the front door. I got something I want to talk to you about anyway."

Red grinned at him foolishly, then started to put the gun away. The punch came at him swiftly. It was short and explosive. If Red had been just a little bit more sober, he would have ducked it. As it was, he almost rolled away from it, revealing how well Kenyatta had trained his people. The blow caught Red on the jaw. He dropped and slowly crumpled up on the floor, knocked completely out.

"I knew it," Charles said from where he sat. "I couldn't believe you were going to let him go in the streets like that."

"I hated to do it," Kenyatta explained to the people watching, "but we got too much to lose to allow him to run around in the streets drunk. If the police get him, no telling what he might say while under the influence of that shit, so it's better all the way around if he stays right here until he's sober."

Kenyatta stopped, reached down, and removed the pistol from the drunken man's coat pocket.

"That's a funky thing to do," Betty said as her whiskey began to talk for her. "Shit, what did Red do to deserve all that?" She glared around angrily. "I don't care if all the rest of these niggers are scared of you, Kenyatta, but I'm sure in the hell not." She belched loudly.

"Shit, Kenyatta," Zeke said from where he sat on the couch nursing his small glass of wine, "looks like you might have another one to go."

"Okay, yeah," she snarled as she staggered around the table to get a better look at Zeke. "Why don't you kill-crazy bastards just kill me, huh? Wouldn't that be the easy way out for all of you? Hell, I know too much for you to let me go on living, don't I? So just shoot me, right here in the top of the head," she said, pointing out the spot.

Her words had brought a snap of fear to most of the people in the room. They were too involved in the robbery to have someone come up with a loose lip. They glanced up at Kenyatta to see how he was taking his woman's words. This could turn into one hell of a dilemma if Kenyatta didn't get her mind right.

He raised his hand, asking for silence. "I know what most of you are thinkin', but forget it. This is the first time any of you have ever seen her drunk, and I promise you it will be the last," he said, not realizing that he was making a promise he would not be able to keep.

"Hey, brother," Robert called out, "we know how it is, man. Just like you said, I ain't never seen Betty loaded before, I mean never. Not even close, man, so I know it's just the drinks in her talking." He spoke with conviction, because he really liked the tall black woman.

"Technically speaking," Eddie-Bee began, loaded

enough himself to start trying to talk proper, which
he did whenever he reached a certain point in his
drinking, "I'd say we've all had a few too many, but
that's why we started drinking, wasn't it? Weren't we
supposed to be celebrating something or other? So
what the fuck. Let's let our hair hang loose. It's exhil-
arating to be loaded around friends." He stopped and
took a large drink from the paper cup in front of him,
then continued. "I'm ready to call the ladies up from
downstairs myself. Let's party, dig? We're not here to
merely exist, are we?" He glared around at his friends,
then spoke to Betty directly. "I really sympathize with
you, Betty. It's getting increasingly boring up here."
He tried to turn his back but only succeeded in knocking his cup of whiskey onto the thick brown carpet.

   The other men laughed. But as Kenyatta took Betty
into his arms, she started a crying jag. At first she
cried softly, then the sobs came louder and louder. He
glanced around at the other men nervously, then
reached down and picked her up and carried her to
the bedroom. Once there, he covered her lips with hot
kisses, holding her tight and slowly rubbing her back
as if she was a nervous filly. She settled down slowly, and he could tell she was coming around and relax-
ing. Her lips grew softer under his, her tongue came
out to meet his until there was nothing but a strong
passion between them. After undressing her with care,
he took her. They made slow and tender love. Her
cries of fear turned into cries of passion.

5

CAPTAIN DAVIDSON STARED over his horn-rimmed glasses at the two officers in front of him. The stout, graying officer realized that it wasn't their fault that none of the officers in homicide had cracked the case yet. At least these two men had come closer to getting an arrest than any of the others. But he still had to crack the whip over their heads, just as he did with the rest of the men.

"Goddamn it, Ryan, Benson, what the hell are you two guys doing back there in your office? Playing with yourselves?" He waited for a second, then continued in a bullish voice. "I can expect nothing from these young college-ass kids I'm stuck with in this

department, but you two guys, shit!" The word came
out in a roar. It could be heard out front, where all
the junior officers worked.

Ryan shifted nervously on his feet. He couldn't
stand being yelled at. It caused his nerves to work
overtime, like they were doing now.

Benson only fought down the smile that threatened
to come to his lips. He realized how nervous Ryan
must be by the loud yelling of their boss. That was
the reason Ryan couldn't stand the interviews. The
yelling just upset him until he couldn't think straight.

Davidson must have realized that he was overdo-
ing it because he lowered his voice. "Now fellows,"
he began, trying another approach, "let's try and look
at it from my side of the wagon, okay? The fuckin'
commissioner is breathing down my neck, cops liter-
ally gettin' killed at will. And now this. Two men with
their girlfriends murdered in cold blood in broad day-
light, yet nobody saw anything. It's unbelievable. I
mean it. We're not back in the roaring twenties. These
things just don't go on in our day and age without
getting solved, so what's the problem? I don't want
to hear about won't nobody talk. I gave you guys a
free hand, allowing you to work when you wanted
to."

He raised his hand to cut off an excuse from Ryan.
"Yeah, I know. You boys were going to work on your
own time. I appreciate the offer, but what did I do? I
said no sirree, not on your own time. Just punch in,
and I'd see to it that you're paid for every fuckin'
minute you put in down here, didn't I?"

Before the men could reply, he continued, and his voice rose higher. "Now, you can't beat such a boss, can you? I put my fat ass out on the limb for you guys. And now they're trying to cut the fuckin' limb off while I'm out on it. But I promise you guys one thing, if they cut it off on me, I'll make damn sure I fall on somebody's head before I hit the ground. Do I make myself clear?"

Both of the officers shook their heads in agreement, thankful that the interview was over and not really bothered by the threat. Before Davidson got rid of them, a hell of a lot of other officers would feel his heavy hand. They were the closest ones to the case. No other team of detectives was anywhere nearer to solving the murder spree than they were.

"Oh, Benson, Ryan," Davidson called out as the two men neared the door in their rush to get clear of the captain's office, "the next time I send you guys two young detectives to take along, please take them. How the hell else are these guys going to get any experience if they don't go with some of you vets?"

"That was my fault, Captain," Benson said quickly. "I...."

The captain waved the excuse away. "I didn't ask about whose fault it was; just take them along next time. I don't see how they can get in the way by just riding in the backseat of a fuckin' police car."

"Okay, Captain, we'll take care of it," Benson replied as he opened the door.

Ryan almost ran through the open door in his haste to get away from the captain. As they made their way through the office, Benson noticed the two young detectives sitting at the desk. Both men were grinnin

The captain waved the excuse away. "I didn't ask atain had said. As Benson caught their eyes, the men glanced away, but not before he could see the look of triumph.

"Up your fuckin' ass," Benson said under his breath. He promised himself that it would be a cold day in hell before he'd allow those bastards to follow him along on any case.

"Hey, Ryan," a slim, red-faced detective called out as they passed, "you and Ben had better check and see if you've still got anything back there to sit on."

The other officers sitting nearby broke out laughing. It tickled them to see another man on the carpet, just as long as it wasn't their own asses catching the hell. To get called into the captain's office wasn't anything to be proud of. He very seldom wanted to see an officer unless it was about something important on a new case, or about someone's mistake.

Benson glared around defiantly at the white officers. It didn't take much for him to realize that they enjoyed what they thought was his being put into place. But a hell of a lot of people had been killed lately, and not only hadn't Ryan and Benson had any luck, but neither had any of the other detectives in the room.

"Let's take a quick ride," Ryan said briskly, not even waiting for his partner's answer. He kept walking until they got in the elevator, then pushed the button for the garage.

Both men remained silent, trying to make some kind of sense out of the latest murders. Ryan drove, taking the freeway until he reached the Clay Street exit. He took the ramp that led to the right and made a turn over to Oakland Avenue. He parked behind a moving van, then removed a small slip of paper from his pocket.

"Kenyatta," he said out loud. "I don't know if he's got anything to do with this shit, but everything we've got leads in his direction."

Benson nodded toward the storefront a few cars away. "Well, that's the bastard's funky-ass club. It took a hell of a lot of trouble just to get somebody to have the nerve to tell us where it was located," Benson stated, then continued. "That in itself speaks of the enormous ghetto power. Whenever people fear somebody, as it seems these people fear him, it's time we looked into it."

Ryan nodded his head in agreement. "I can't understand how this guy exploded in our midst without us ever gettin' any kind of wire on him. It's as if he came from another world. Nobody, and I mean nobody, wants to talk about him or his people."

As the two detectives sat watching the front of the club, a small black Ford pulled up. The car was tilted over towards the driver's seat, and when the driver got out, it was easy to see why. A huge, fat, white man got out from the driver's side and waddled around the car, carrying a brown briefcase in his left hand. He glanced down at a piece of paper in his right hand, reading an address as he reached the sidewalk.

The three black men loitering in front of the building stared at him coldly as he pushed past them. He was breathing hard as though he had just run ten miles.

"I wonder who the hell he could be," Benson said quietly.

Ryan lifted his shoulders in a shrug. "He could be the neighborhood's friendly insurance man, you know." Even while he was talking, Ryan was writing down the license number of the late-model car.

As Benson watched his partner write down the number, he couldn't help but think how it would be if the fat white man had been black. His partner probably would have suggested that they pull him over when he came out and shake him down.

For spite, Benson started to make the suggestion himself. Why not, he thought coldly. What's good for a black man should be good for a white one, too. But he knew better. If the white man turned out to be a working businessman going about his business of robbing the black neighborhood and they shook him down, all he'd have to do would be to call downtown and make a complaint about being illegally stopped and searched. Then there would be hell to pay. They would have to come up with some kind of an excuse for why they had detained the man and put him through so much trouble.

Benson had to laugh sardonically as he thought about it: all those black men who were stopped daily, even with their wives along, and searched out on the streets for no other reason than that they were black. The officers who stopped them believed all black men did something wrong, so they had a right to stop and frisk any black man they saw. But it was so different when it came to a white man. *Oh God, so much different*, he moaned.

"What's wrong?" Ryan inquired slowly, studying his partner closely. "You got an idea or something?"

For just a minute Benson debated with himself on whether or not to let his partner in on his private little joke.

Defiantly he stated, "Oh man, do you really want to know?" He then continued before Ryan could answer, "I was thinking, Ryan, why go through the trouble of writing his number down, then havin' to check it downtown, when more than fuckin' likely it's a rented car in a phony name? To beat all that shit, why don't we just act like he's a black dude when he comes out and lean on him a little. You know what I mean, Ryan? We lean on enough niggers daily for it to be quite easy."

Benson watched his partner's face. It went red, then Ryan rubbed at his chin nervously, trying to make up his mind on how to answer Benson.

"Man, you're really in a hell of a mood today, huh?" Ryan began as he thought over the ticklish question Benson had dropped in his lap. He cursed silently at himself, wishing he had left well enough alone. Now, since he'd asked for it, Benson had really put it in his lap. All of the problems of what could happen flashed through his mind. The last thing he wanted was another meeting with the captain—not anytime soon anyway. If the fat salesman was to do any complaining, that's just what it would add up to. Another fuckin' meeting with the captain. There was something like a tacit agreement among the policemen about white businessmen. You didn't harass them while they were down in the black neighborhoods. A white junkie was something else. He was nothing. But a taxpayer, that was a horse of another color—white color at that.

Benson could read it all in his face. "Don't worry, Ryan, I was just foolin' with you, man. I don't want the trouble it could bring either."

For a minute Ryan couldn't look his partner in the eye. "You make me feel like a three-dollar bill, Ben. If you want to, we can shake him down. I was just thinking, though, if a kickback comes out of this shit, we'll have some tall explaining to do. The fuckin' captain will say, 'Why are you guys hustling a white man? Everybody in the city knows it was black gunmen who made the hit, so where's the connection with this white merchant?'"

He didn't have to illustrate too much for Benson to know that his partner was right. "I mean, Ben," Ryan added, "it won't go as hard for me as it could go for you. All I'd have to say was that it was your idea and I just went along with it, even though you know I wouldn't shift the blame on you. But I'm just trying to show you where we'd be. The first thing we'd have to answer is why. Why in the fuck did we bother him? Don't we have enough troublemakers down here to cope with without going out of our way to disturb workin' people?"

The very air in the car seemed to become oppressive to Benson, but what his partner said was true. They would never be able to make their superiors understand. Even as Benson thought about it, it seemed foolish. What would a well-dressed white man want with someone like Kenyatta, except to sell him something that would be junk a month later? They lived in two different worlds; the world of men like Kenyatta was a black world, devoid of whites. Even as Benson thought about it, he remembered that the little he was able to dig up on Kenyatta showed him to be militant, preaching against associating with whites. As he went over the possibilities in his mind, Benson quickly came to the conclusion that the fat white man was probably just the landlord coming to collect his rent.

He put his thoughts into words. "You know, Ryan, I'm grabbing at straws, really. That guy's probably the landlord trying to collect his rent." Benson laughed dryly, then added, "And that's more than likely one hell of a job right there, trying to get his rent out of a bunch of hustlers like them punks hanging out there. Yeah, he's got one hell of a job on his hands, if I know anything about young brothers."

Ryan wasn't fooled by his partner's words. It had hurt Benson to make that small confession. Benson really wanted to shake down the white man. "Now, Ben, don't go against your hunches. If you want to, just give the word, man, and we'll have that fat load of lard jacked up before God gets the news."

"You're a good man, Ryan," Benson said slowly.

"Yeah, you're a damn good one to work with. But now that I think about it, I believe I was wrong. I can't picture no reason for there to be any connection between them, other than legal business. Kenyatta hates whites, so they couldn't have much other than business between them. Let's let it pass this time. We can still check out the license number with headquarters."

6

THE BLACK MEN SHUFFLED reluctantly out of Kenyatta's private office. None of them wanted to leave until they found out what the fat white man wanted. It was the first time any of them had ever seen Kenyatta treat a white man with any kind of respect. When this one entered, Kenyatta had gotten up and walked across the carpeted floor to throw his arm around the fat man's shoulders as if they were old war buddies. After making the man as comfortable as possible, Kenyatta had started ushering the rest of the people out of the office until there wasn't anyone left but him and the white man.

"Well, Angelo," Kenyatta began, "I hope you

brought what I wanted."

Angelo rubbed his hand across his huge stomach. He had been nervous at the sight of so many young, wild-looking black men. He knew they were follow-ers of Kenyatta, and that Kenyatta preached death to the white man. So far, though, all he'd received was the red-carpet treatment.

Before answering the question Kenyatta had put to him, he asked one of his own. "What about the paper? You know what I mean, that green stuff." Angelo leaned across the desk on his elbows and tried to stare Kenyatta in the eye but quickly changed his mind. Instead he tried to cover up his error by playing the big shot.

"I don't generally come this far out of my way for no fuckin' body, Kenny," he stated, glaring across the desk, "but you've been bugging me for this informa-tion for the past six months at least, so I come up with it for you, but I've got to have my bread."

Kenyatta stared coldly at the nervous white man. Suddenly he stood up from behind his desk. "Listen, sucker," he began loudly, "you come down here and I try and treat you like a man, but that ain't good enough for you. You want us to kiss your fuckin' ass to show how much we appreciate your coming *down* here, as you say. But we ain't doing nothing of the kind. Honky, you came *down* here because you can't sell that information you got nowhere else in this world. Ain't nobody willin' to pay the price I was goin' pay for it."

Angelo drew a deep breath, letting it out slowly,

hoping the tightness he felt would disappear with it. He hadn't missed the past tense Kenyatta had used. The words seemed to stifle the very air in the room. He pulled at his collar, and his face became red as a beet. The glare coming from the ceiling lights seemed to move the walls inward, sealing him in. He could picture the army of people he was in debt to, marching arm in arm toward him, each one carrying a different kind of weapon.

"Now wait a minute, boy," he began, and realized at once that he had blundered before he even began. That was the problem of trying to deal with these fuckin' spades. You couldn't open your mouth without steppin' on their tender egos some kind of way.

Kenyatta's voice was smooth and softly triumphant. "Things have just changed a little, that's all, Angelo. We don't have to pay that wild price you were asking now because we already know half of the names ourselves. But," Kenyatta waved to the man to remain silent, "since you did go through so much trouble, we've decided to offer you five thousand dollars for your snitching. I mean, if you really look at it like you should, that's good money for an informer, whether he's white or black."

Being called an informer didn't set too well with Angelo either, but what hurt worse than that was the thought that he couldn't collect the whole ten thousand dollars he had come to think of as his own. Yet five grand was better than nothing. As far as he was concerned, the information he was passing on to these black guys was less than useless. He couldn't see what they could possibly do with it. Even if they turned it over to the police, it would be nothing new. The big wheels in the police department already knew who was responsible for the steady flow of dope into the city, yet they couldn't, or wouldn't, do anything about it. So what could some black hoods living in a ghetto do?

Angrily he reached in his pocket and snatched out the envelope. "Here," he snarled as he tossed it across the desk, all the time hoping that the black man wouldn't change his mind again. He needed the five grand to live. Without it, he was a walking dead man. His mind was already working on how he could pay certain people half their money. When they saw him come up with some cash, they would know that he was trying, that he wasn't just attempting to shine them on. Yes, the five grand would be enough to hold back the strong-arm boys.

Kenyatta stared at the envelope as if it was a snake. He hadn't appreciated the white man tossing it down on his desk instead of handing it to him like a man. For a second, he visualized himself choking the fat man to death. It was a picture that he enjoyed. How desperately the fat man would struggle. The image of the man's red face turning blue brought a smile to his lips.

Angelo sat impatiently waiting for Kenyatta to make up his mind. Nervously he lit up a fat cigar. "I mean, what the hell gives around here, Kenyatta? We ain't never had any kind of misunderstanding like this before. I bring you what you ask for, but you've changed the fuckin' price. How the hell will you feel if I should do the same thing to you the next time you put in a big order for guns, huh?"

It didn't take a mind reader to see that he had hit on a vital organ. The steady supply of fresh, untraceable guns was indispensable. It was of the greatest importance that Kenyatta keep his gun connection. Angelo saw this and pushed home his point. "You and me, Kenyatta, we been doing business for over two years now, without ever having any trouble. Now, all at once, here comes some bullshit. Okay, I accept the fact that ten grand was too much money for the information you wanted, but don't rub my nose in shit, boy."

There it was again, that fuckin' term "boy." Kenyatta gritted his teeth before jumping up and stalking around the desk. "Angelo, I'm goin' tell you one time, man, and only once. The way you honkies have of calling us 'boy' is too much. I'm one nigger who just can't stand it. Now, I know you probably don't mean a fuckin' thing by it, but it still rubs me to the quick to hear a peckerwood call me 'boy,' so you done run out of chances. If you do it again, no matter how bad I might need your gun connect, I'll personally kick you in your fat ass until all the lard runs off it."

All the while the tall black man spoke, he pointed his finger down into the white man's face. Angelo could only sit in the chair and stare up at him with his mouth open. He promised himself though, if he got out of that office alive, it would be a cold day in hell before he'd ever come down near the ghetto and do business with the black bastards again. Oh yes, he'd continue to sell them guns. It made him feel good to know that he was supplying the guns they were killing each other with. In time, maybe they'd kill so many of their brothers that the white people could start getting back some parts of the cities because, the way things stood, niggers had already taken over the major portions.

"I didn't mean no harm, Kenyatta; it's just that I forget how to pronounce your name at times and 'boy' comes out. But don't worry, I won't make that mistake again."

Kenyatta glared down at the man without smiling. "I ain't worried about it at all," Kenyatta said. "I've already warned you; the rest is up to you." He turned his back on the fat man and walked back around his desk. This time he did pick up the envelope. He opened it quickly, glanced down at the names, then back up at Angelo. "What kind of shit is this you're giving me, Angelo? You got the Kingfisher in charge of the dope on the west side, east side, north side, and south side of the city. In other words, you got a black man in charge of all the dope that goes into the ghettos."

Angelo held up his hand, catching himself before he made the mistake of calling Kenyatta boy. "It's the goddamn truth. I was surprised as hell when I found it out. I didn't know a nigger had that much power." He became tongue-tied as he suddenly realized the word he had used, but since no warning came he continued. "It's the truth though. Kingfisher has the whole ball of wax. There's not a white distributor in the whole fuckin' city who can put any dope in the ghettos without the okay of the Kingfisher."

Angelo's words rang in Kenyatta's ears. "That's the way that bastard has got it set up. No drugs are sold on the large levels unless he has something to do with it. It's no big outlet in the suburbs yet, so the big boys have to play to the Kingfisher's tune for now. They damn sure don't like it, but what can they do about it? There's not another colored guy around anywhere as big as the Kingfisher. He don't allow it. If the big white boys try and set up another black guy, something always seems to happen to the guy. It's a short investment, so they have to do business with the Kingfisher."

The spectacle of watching the facial expressions of Kenyatta was enough to scare the shit out of some people, and Angelo was no exception. At first Kenyatta had been defiant, then uncontrolled fury flashed across his features. Just the mention of the Kingfisher was enough to make Angelo wish he was somewhere else.

"Well," Angelo began, "I'd appreciate it if we closed our little business deal, because I've got to get uptown and check on a shipment of guns. You do still want that big order, don't you?" It was clear he was trying desperately to change the subject.

With difficulty Kenyatta managed to bring his mind back to the business at hand. A blinding white rage had blotted out all his thoughts for a moment, until the only thing he could think about was revenge.

But the guns were of immediate concern to him. Without them, he couldn't begin to put into practice any of the far-reaching plans he had. It took a few seconds but he managed to gain control of his anger.

"Yeah, Angelo, I know where you're coming from. Just hold on to your shirt for a minute, man," he said, as he reached inside his pocket and removed an envelope. He took his time and counted out the money on the desk. Angelo counted the money alongside him, not even attempting to keep the greed out of his eyes.

"Why don't you give me a partial payment down on the guns now, Ken, and tomorrow night when you send your people over to pick them up, they won't have to have that much cash on them." Angelo's eyes continued to follow the large roll of money still inside the envelope.

Kenyatta laughed loudly. "Man, you must really need some bread bad, Angelo. Suppose I did what you asked me to do, then something happened during the pickup. I'd be out of my money, plus the guns. No, baby, ain't no way for it to go like that. I couldn't stand to lose on both ends. It would hurt me bad enough if the cops knocked off our pickup spot, but it would ruin me if I lost all my bankroll along with it." The tall, lean, black man stood up from behind his desk, showing by his actions that the interview was over. He walked around the desk and took Angelo's arm, leading the white man toward the door. "To show you how much I'm concerned about you, Angelo, I'm even going to walk you out to your car so that there won't be no chance of somebody knockin' you off for the few bucks you just picked up. I don't want no shit out of you, you know what I mean? Like you calling me back in an hour tellin' me some shit about somebody knockin' you over. Well, baby, I'm goin' make damn sure that don't happen."

The black man's deep laughter boomed out loudly as they went through the outer office. Neither man took notice of the black men standing around in the room.

Near the front window, two Negro men stood peeping out. One of them yelled out to Kenyatta before he opened the front door. "Hey, baby, maybe you had better be cool. It's a couple of detectives parked down the street. They been there ever since fat boy pulled up and parked. At first we thought they might have been a couple of his boys, you know, trying to put a little protection on him, but we checked them out and it's them two detectives from homicide. The black and white cops that always work together."

Kenyatta stopped with his hand on the door, undecided on which course to take. "You say they been down there checkin' out the place, huh?" he asked, his mind racing.

"Naw," the tall, angular black man called Jug replied. "Naw, I didn't say they were checkin' out our joint. I said they seemed to be checkin' out fat boy's car."

As Jug talked, Angelo stared at the black man. He shook his head. They did all look alike, only this one had hair. If he cut off his hair, he'd probably look just like Kenyatta, Angelo reasoned quietly.

It was true to a certain extent. Kenyatta and Jug were almost the same height; both men had the same lean build, with wide shoulders tapering down to a small waist—men built for power, speed, and explosive action.

"Goddamn it, Kenyatta, I told you you should have come downtown and picked up that shit. Now I'm involved down here with the fuckin' police. It's been years, man, since I've had a run-in with a cop. Now, I don't need this kind of shit, but what am I going to do? I sure in the fuck can't sit here at your place all fuckin' day."

It was the man's tone of voice that rubbed him wrong. Now, even though the law was outside, Kenyatta wanted to get rid of the fat white man. He glanced over his shoulder, then snapped his fingers.

"Betty!" he ordered, his voice full of wrath.

The tall black woman came running across the room.

"Honey, I want you to walk this honky out to his car, put your arm around him, you know, give the impression that he just finished knockin' off some black pussy. The cops are down the block and we would like to fake them out, so make it look good."

She glanced up at him in surprise. "Okay, honey, you know I wanna do whatever you want me to."

It was clear to everybody looking that what Betty was doing was something Kenyatta sure in the hell didn't like. He had to turn his back when she took Angelo's arm and went out the door.

Kenyatta stalked back to his office and slammed

the door. He didn't want to be bothered by anyone. Kenyatta gritted his teeth so hard his jaw hurt. It was the first time he'd ever had to use his woman in such a way. He'd rather have had her kill Angelo than walk out pretending that the fat man was her lover.

Betty led the fat man outside. She put her arm around his huge waist and held him close. She sniffed, then tried to hold her breath. There was an odor about the heavy man that was repugnant to her. It would have been farcical for her to pretend that she didn't smell him, because she couldn't hide her reaction. She pulled away from him quickly, even though she still kept her arm around his waist. But one glance at her face, with her nose turned up, would have been enough for anyone to see the dislike on it.

As obvious as it was, it went unnoticed by Angelo. He was too concerned with the police car parked down the street. He fumbled in his pockets until he found his car keys, then he attempted to make a convivial social impression for the officers watching. He puckered up his ruddy pink lips and tried to kiss Betty, but she wasn't having any of it. She didn't even want the man to kiss her on the cheek. She broke away from his embrace.

"It don't take all that," she stated coldly as she backed away from him, still smiling and grinning. The smile never touched her cold black eyes.

"Well, I'll be a sonofabitch," Benson growled harshly. "Here we fuck up half the morning waiting on this bastard, and all the time he's upstairs playing house with one of Kenyatta's whores!"

Ryan cursed loudly too. "It looks that way, don't it. He probably came to collect the rent and the broad gave him some cunt for the rent money."

The two detectives watched the fat man drive past them slowly. It seemed as if he was trying to remove some lipstick from his cheek with a hankie as he went past.

"Well, what now?" Ryan asked quietly, deep in thought. Something was wrong, but for the moment he couldn't seem to put his finger on it.

"I don't know," Benson replied. "Maybe it would be better if we went on in. I think I'll go home and have some sleep. We seem to be too close to something not to be gettin' any answers."

Ryan shook his head. "It's right before us, Ben, but for some damn reason we can't see it. Maybe you're right. After some rest, we might be able to think better. Drop me off at my place, will you?"

Benson nodded his head in agreement. "I'll pick you back up tonight, say around ten o'clock." Neither man bothered to speak again until Benson pulled up on Carpenter Street and let his partner out.

"We missed something, Ben," Ryan stated, shaking his head. "I don't know what the fuck it was, but I just got the feelin' that something escaped us that shouldn't have."

"Maybe," Benson replied. "After you sleep on it, it might come to you." He grinned, then put the car in gear and pulled away from the curb. Even as he drove, the same thought kept nagging him; then it hit him like a ton of bricks.

Kenyatta was a black militant. There was no way in the world he would allow one of his black women to try turning a trick with a honky. They just wouldn't do it. His group preached against the white man, so it had been all a fake-out—something to fool the two foolish cops sitting down the street.

He slammed on his brakes and made a U-turn. It was too important to pass up. Ryan had the license number of the fat man's car, and he needed it. It looked as if there wouldn't be much sleep that afternoon for either one of the detectives. This clue was too good to pass up, and the case was too hot to not follow up each and every fucking thing they got their hands on.

When he pulled up in front of Ryan's house, he just blew on the horn. In seconds his partner came out of the freshly painted white house.

Ryan must have sensed something, because he ran down the battleship-gray-colored steps. When he reached the car, he didn't bother with just putting his head through the open window. He opened the door and got in. In a second, Benson explained why he had come back.

As Benson talked, Ryan nodded his head up and down. "I knew it," the man exploded. "It was there, right there before us, but neither one of us could put our finger on it at the time. Well, quit wasting time. Let's get downtown. This fat bastard had better be clean, 'cause we're going to do a lot of checkin' up on his ass."

7

AS KENYATTA STARED at the death list in his hands he could feel a thrill of exhilaration racing through his veins. Now they could do more than just merely exist. The five grand he had paid out for it was nothing. Money meant very little to him anyway. It was just a tool, something to use to gain the things he wanted for his people. Now they could begin to move against the dope pushers, the ones who supplied the city, not just the neighborhood pushers who sold dope to take care of their own drug habits.

He glanced around the apartment. He had sent out the word and the people were arriving. Loud, raucous laughter came from the front room, where a group of people waited. It was time, and everybody could sense it. The members were in a happy, responsive mood. Kenyatta had sent out the word that they were to meet at the ranch and everybody was moving to the country again.

There was a cacophony of sound coming from the people in all the rooms. It was an atmosphere of social gaiety as everybody looked forward to the trip. Some cars had already left so that things would be ready when the main party arrived at the farm.

Betty sat on the arm rest of the overstuffed chair in the living room next to Kenyatta, smiling broadly at everybody.

"Eddie-Bee," Kenyatta called out loudly. "Hey, Eddie-Bee, I thought you took the station wagon around to Johnnie's to get the starter fixed on it."

"I did, baby, I did, but wasn't no reason for me to sit around there and wait for them to finish workin' on it. Johnnie said he'd call as soon as he finished workin' on it and that Buick he's puttin' a muffler on. I told him we wanted both of them finished as soon as goddamn possible, so he said to give him thirty or forty minutes and he'd have them together for us."

Kenyatta replied by flashing Eddie-Bee one of his most indulgent smiles. "My man," he said loudly, "that's what I dig about the brothers in this organization. Ain't no bullshit about them. All of you have been trained. You're together, ready to cope with the white man, while the other brothers out in the streets are still blinded by the white man's shit."

As he talked, Kenyatta raised his voice into a lecturing tone. "Each and every one of you in this room right now has been trained until you're like a machine—dangerous to those who try to handle you and handle you wrong."

The people in the room fell silent, listening to their leader. What he said was the truth. Each and every one of them were trained killers, the women as well as the men. There was not a person inside the building who wouldn't kill a white or even a black person if Kenyatta so ordered it. They were all assassins, trained in the art of death.

Even the tall, attractive black woman who sat at his elbow could murder women or children if the need arose. Kenyatta had trained his small band of disciples so well that there was no feeling of guilt over an act of violence, no matter how brutal it might be. Whatever they did was justified as an application of justice—black justice. It was the only kind of justice that held any significant meaning to any of them. That white justice was a mockery could be seen openly every day in the courtrooms—used for the rich and forced on the poor.

"Red has gone to the farm," Kenyatta continued. Everybody was listening quietly to what he had to say. "I sent him and his lady on out with another couple. They took most of the guns with them, so we won't have to worry about transporting our weapons. I'm not sure, but the police may have been watching the place. When I say I'm not sure, I mean I don't have any idea why they would bother to go through the trouble of watching us. We ain't doing nothing." His words brought laughter from his listeners.

Slowly, like a well-trained actor, Kenyatta raised his hand for silence. "I don't want to get into it real deep right now, but we got what we been waitin' for. I got the names of some of the biggest honkies in the fuckin' city. I'm talkin' about the motherfuckin' honkies who have been living out in Grosse Pointe, while selling dope down in the center city. Of course they don't have to come down here and sell it themselves, 'cause they got a good head nigger who goes by the name of Kingfisher. But once we knock Kingfisher's ass off, they goin' have mighty big trouble findin' another good nigger like him!"

There was a roar like the sea makes when it's beginning an angry storm. The storm was brewing right there in that small apartment. It had started to brew many years ago, before many of the dedicated young blacks were even born.

Zeke, the tall, light-brown-complexioned man who had been in on the holdup with Red, spoke up. "It's damn sure time, Ken," he stated, using the short nickname that only a few of Kenyatta's closest friends ever used.

There was the sound of the rear doorbell ringing. Instantly the people in the apartment became silent, each wondering who would be using the alley entrance. To get up the rear steps, a person had to come through the alley, then walk through a trash-littered garage, which led into the small enclosure that was the backyard. After getting to the yard, they could only come up on the rear porch and ring the back doorbell. The stairway that led upstairs was enclosed, so that somebody had to go down the back steps to unlock the door.

The people waited quietly to see who was coming up. Betty moved uneasily on her perch as the newcomer approached. As the man entered, everybody there recognized him. He was the kind of person who would be recognized in a crowd. His arrival caused a different kind of reaction in each person there, but the women reacted the most. Betty was not the only woman who moved back in fear.

The man wore a long black coat that was wrapped around him like a cloak, covering a tall, very spare body. Beneath the rounded dome of a closely shaved skull, large black eyes peered from either side of a jutting, beak-like nose. The mouth below was sunken, the lips puckered, and the chin had a sharp upward hook. With one dark brown hand the man caressed the bony line of his jaw, staring coldly around at the people in the room. Under the probing of those lusterless black eyes, each person either waved at him feebly or glanced away as if they hadn't noticed his searching stare. The atmosphere in the room changed. It was as if something unclean, something foul with slime, had crept amongst them.

Kenyatta seemed as if he was the only person in the room who hadn't noticed the change. "What's happenin', Creeper?" he asked, as Creeper stopped in front of him.

Betty quickly got up from her perch on the side of the chair and walked back towards the kitchen. "I think I'll get a drink. You want one, daddy?" she asked over her shoulder.

"Naw, baby, I don't want anything, but Creeper might care for a drink." He glanced up at the man. As their gaze met, Kenyatta experienced a shrinking inner horror. This man was something he did not and could not understand. He was a man who was totally alien to his own world. The Creeper was one of the oldest members of his organization. He wasn't dedicated to any cause except Kenyatta, and only because Kenyatta had saved his life. He had been shot and wounded by the police, trying to find a hiding place in an alley, when Kenyatta had found him and taken him home, cared for his wound, then gave him a place to live. For that help, the tall black man called "the Creeper" had become like a shadow to Kenyatta.

"Well, what will it be, Creeper?" Betty asked, not trying to hide the dislike in her voice.

"Did I ask for anything?" Creeper replied, then turned his back on her as if she wasn't there. For some strange reason, out of all the people in Kenyatta's organization, Betty was the only one that Creeper really hated. Even he couldn't understand the intensity of his hatred for the woman. He blamed her for coming between him and Kenyatta, but it went deeper than that. He had never cared for another human being in his life. Then Kenyatta had come to his rescue. It was not just the help either, it was the way the other man treated him—like a man. Kenyatta didn't turn away from him in horror because of his looks. He'd been aware for years of his looks since he'd been a child, when kids had started calling him "the Creeper" because of the similarity of his features to those of the man who played the Creeper in the movies. In time, he'd come to accept it, not caring one way or another what they called him. He was a man who lived alone, until he met Kenyatta.

The man stood over Kenyatta until Kenyatta grew uneasy. "Well, what is it, brother? You seem to have something on your mind but you ain't saying nothing."

For an answer, Creeper let his eyes roam over the other people in the room. "You know me better than to think I'd say anything in front of them," he replied, loud enough for everybody to hear. "The first time one of these niggers gets uptight, they goin' blow this whole fuckin' thing up in your face, Kenyatta, you just wait and see."

Before Kenyatta could give an answer to that, Creeper let his coat slip open. "I took care of that little thing you asked me to handle for you," he stated harshly, not bothering to rebutton his coat.

For a minute Kenyatta couldn't think. The man standing in front of him was covered with blood. *What was the man talking about*, Kenyatta asked himself. He remembered asking the man to check up on Kingfisher's right-hand man, but other than that, he couldn't remember asking him to take care of anything.

Kenyatta rose from his chair in one smooth motion and beckoned with his head. "Come on," he said, leading the way towards the bedroom. He wanted to get to the bottom of this, and the sooner the better. Something had happened, and whatever it was, blood had been spilled.

Across town in his penthouse apartment, the Kingfisher moved around like a man struck down by an unknown force. The information that had just come to him was so shocking that he couldn't believe it. The Kingfisher was used to death but not when it was an act of gross mutilation so close to home.

As Kingfisher paced back and forth in his penthouse apartment, he kept murmuring to himself. "Too close, too fuckin' close to home…, if they can knock off my right-hand man." He shook his head, unnerved to his very roots by this murderous act.

8

AFTER THE BRUTAL DEATHS of Kenyatta's people by Kingfisher's hit men, Kenyatta had called one person in and given him one assignment: find out which ones were responsible, then handle it if you can. It hadn't taken the man that long to find out who had given the order, and when he reported back that it was the Kingfisher, he was then given another order. If you can't get the big fish, get the next biggest fish in the pond. Even that order proved quite hard to do. The next biggest fish was Kingfisher's right-hand man, Sam. Sam was as hard to reach as the Kingfisher—almost.

It took a while for the Creeper to find the weak

link. He had the uncanny ability of being able to pry into things that ordinary men would have long given up on. The Creeper believed that every man had a weakness, somewhere; all you had to do was search for it, and eventually it would come to light.

In the case of the Kingfisher's right-hand man and trusted personal bodyguard, Sam, the truth wasn't too hard to dig up. Once the Creeper found out that Sam had a wife, two girls, and a four-year-old boy, it was just a matter of time. The man who had helped order the death of four members of Kenyatta's organization would eventually show up at his home. Only the Creeper didn't have the patience to wait until Sam decided to pay his wife and kids a visit. He decided to hurry the matter up. Having already been given his orders, he didn't bother to check back with Kenyatta. He did to the best of his ability just what had been asked of him.

Mary, the woman who had made the mistake of bearing two children for Sam, knew nothing of Sam's business. All she knew was that he made a good living. He was the first black man she had ever lived with who took care of her and her children so well that she never worried about money problems. Whenever she needed money, she just called Sam and explained to him what she needed it for and how much. It didn't really matter that she didn't have a marriage license; Sam took care of her better than the man she had married earlier in her life. That marriage hadn't lasted but two years, and in those two years she caught more hell than the average woman ran into in a lifetime. But the marriage had been legal. She kept the proof of her first marriage locked up in an iron chest in the closet, but she didn't really need it. The two girls who belonged to Sam were more proof than any piece of paper could ever be.

Her two girls by Sam were both born out of wedlock but, as far as she was concerned, Sam was her husband even though they had never gone before a preacher. He was good to all of his children. Whenever he bought something for the girls, he made sure he brought the boy something too. The girls, one three and the other fifteen months, were treated like small dolls by their father whenever he had the time to be around them. Most of the time he wasn't home, but he made sure they never wanted for anything. It was one of the few joys Sam really got out of life, buying things for the kids—things that he wasn't able to have when he was a child because of money problems.

The small family lived happily in this manner until the day that Mary saw a strange man bringing her son David home. The man was monstrous and ugly. Mary wondered how the preschool could allow such a person to work for them, but at once she regretted her thoughts. Even this human being had to live. It was for sure he hadn't made himself, so who was she to complain about his looks. Overwhelmed by pity, she opened her door wide, allowing the man who clutched her struggling son to enter.

"What did he do at school?" she managed to ask as they entered the house. "Do you have to hold him so roughly?" she inquired, as David tried to twist out of the vicious hold the man had on his arm. Tears rolled from David's eyes, even after the man released him. The man glanced around the house.

He noticed the expensive carpet on the floor and the dark brown wall-to-wall fabric that matched the golden colored furnishings. The couch and matching chair, the marble coffee table, the solid marble end tables, all gave an idea of the good life that was being lived here.

"Oh, Sam don't do too bad for himself, do he?" the man inquired. His voice was low and carried a sharp note in it.

At the mention of Sam, Mary's heart seemed to freeze. She realized at once this wasn't something her son had done at school. The man had used David as an excuse to get inside the house. *Oh, my God,* she thought to herself. Suddenly the baby girl started crying in her playpen, which was kept right in the front room.

As she started to go to the child, she said, "There must be some mistake somewhere. This Sam you're talking about, he doesn't live here."

She had to pass between the man and the coffee table to reach the child. He reached out and pushed her back.

"If I were you, honey child," Creeper said coldly, "I wouldn't worry too much about that child crying."

"Well, you don't happen to be me!" Mary yelled at him as she attempted to jerk her arm free.

What happened then seemed more like a dream to

her than reality. It had been so long since someone had put their hands on her. His hand came up slowly, or so it seemed to Mary, and he slapped her across the face twice.

"Now, honey child," he began in that same singsong voice, "I want you to cooperate with me." Seeing the defiant look come into her eyes, he grinned. "This is no joke, girl. If you love your kids, you will do just what I ask of you."

He shoved her down on the couch, causing her housecoat to fly up, but she paid small heed to that. If rape was all the man wanted, she was willing if only he'd get it over with and leave—leave just like he came, without really harming anyone. But in the back of her mind she knew it wouldn't be that simple. This man wasn't interested in fucking her. She could sense something monstrous and grotesque about him, an evil that she couldn't completely grasp.

Shuddering with repugnance she managed to ask, "What is it you want?"

"Why, child, I've already told you. Sam. I want the big shot, Sam the man." His laughter came then, cold, chilling, frightening.

She tried again. "Please, I've already told...." The lie froze in her throat. The man had produced a straight razor from his pocket and opened it quickly.

"That's right, child," he said in that same funny tone. "I'm not here to play games. Now, if you keep lying, I'm going to cut that boy's throat right in front of you."

Could this be true? Could it really be happening?

She wanted to pinch herself to see if she was asleep.
Mary tried to close and reopen her eyes. It was just
too much to believe. The man couldn't possibly be so
bloodthirsty as to kill her son. The very thought of it
was too much for her mind to accept.

"Please!" She made a small feeble gesture with her
hand, trying to express what she couldn't find the
words to say. She still couldn't believe that the man
would hurt her child. "Listen, I don't have any way
to reach Sam. He calls me."

The words were hardly out of her mouth before the
man went into action. He didn't waste any time. It
was as if he were butchering a cow. He snatched the
small boy to him and drew the sharp razor across the
boy's throat before she realized what had happened.
The quick flow of blood that came from the wound
brought her to her senses. The man pushed the boy
away and the small child fell onto the floor.

An animal cry of pain came from the woman then,
as she stumbled down beside the child. There was
nothing she could do. As she clutched the child to her,
his life's blood ran out in her lap. From the floor she
glared up at the Creeper, shocked almost out of her
mind.

"One down and two to go," he said in a quiet voice
as he moved over towards the little girl in the playpen.
She was still a toddler. She stood there looking up at
the man with her arms outstretched for him to pick
her up.

Something deep down inside Mary warned her that
her anguish would have to be controlled if she want-

ed to save the rest of her family. "Please, no more," she cried, "I'll call him." With those words she started to weep. The outburst was not convulsive but sheer grief. A grief that would never find that gratifying relief in tears.

"Mommie, Mommie," the dark-haired three-year-old cried, "what's wrong, Mommie?"

Mary pulled the child to her, her arms gripping the child tightly. Mary was a tall woman in her late twenties. Built heavy from delivering babies, she now had the body of a woman—a big woman. Large arms that spoke of strength—she was a woman who could work in the fields beside her man if it was ever necessary.

The little child with the pigtails running down each side of her head began to cry. She wanted the tall man beside her to reach down and pick her up.

Impatiently, the Creeper reached down and rubbed the child's head. In his other hand he held the bloody razor. Mary glanced up from where she was kneeling, her heart almost stopping.

"Please," she begged, "I'll call, I'll call." Her hands groped wildly for the phone. "Get mommie the phone," she said to the small child beside her. The little girl ran off at once, pulling the telephone off the end table and dragging it back toward her crying mother. Tears continued to run down Mary's cheeks, but no sound came out. She knew the little boy she held in her lap was gone. Now the only thing she could hope for was to save her girls. Sam, big, strong Sam—he would know how to handle this madman! The thought flashed through her mind as she tried to remember the number he had given her to call in case of an emergency. Desperately she dialed the number, only to find out that she had called the wrong one. She stopped and tried to get her mind right. She had to think right. She fought down the desire to throw herself against the madman. It would be useless. No matter how strong she was, there was something about the man that spoke of pure danger. Even as fear-ridden as she was, she wondered if Sam would be able to do anything with him. She couldn't see this skinny man being able to contain all that strength. No, Sam would handle him when he got here.

Apprehension filled her very soul as she watched the man stroke her child's head. "Please, leave the baby alone," she managed to say. "I'm making your call for you, so just leave my child alone."

The man's hand stopped in mid-air. "Okay, dear," he said softly, as he turned away from the playpen. "Just get the call through."

Vaguely she heard another voice on the other end of the phone. "Sam," she blurted out, "I've got to speak to Sam!" It took a few seconds, then she heard his strong voice on the line. She blurted out something about one of the children being hurt, then begged him to come home at once so that he could rush the child to the hospital.

The message got across to Sam. He made a hurried excuse to Kingfisher and left.

If there was one thing Sam didn't want, it was one of his hood friends ever coming in contact with his family. For some reason, he believed if he kept his friends away there would never be any problem. None of the dirt that he dealt in would rub off. He would have been hard pressed to explain it himself if asked, but either way he made sure none of his friends ever visited him while he was staying with Mary.

For a brief moment after Sam left, Kingfisher was undecided on whether or not he should have some of the boys follow him. But just as quickly as the notion came into his head, he dismissed it. Sam was his most trusted man, and if he couldn't trust Sam, who the hell could he trust? Later he was to regret having made that decision, for if he had followed through with it, he might have been able to put an end to his troubles right then and there.

It took Sam less than thirty minutes to reach his beautiful red-brick home in Conant Gardens, a black neighborhood that only the blacks with above-average incomes could buy into. He pulled into the driveway. As he jumped out and ran for the front door, he was surprised that Mary hadn't come out to meet him. The woman was able to carry the child just as well as he was, and if it was as serious as she said, she would have been waiting for him at the door.

As he ran across the well-kept lawn he noticed the front door was cracked halfway open. He jumped up on the porch and didn't stop until he had burst through the front door. Then he stopped abruptly. At first he couldn't believe his eyes. His mind didn't want to accept what he saw. He wiped his eyes with the back of his hand, only to find the sight still there when he reopened them. The first thing that came to his sight was his baby daughter, her pen pushed in front of the front door so that whoever entered would have to walk around it to get into the front room. The small child lay out on the clean mattress, clean except for the dried blood around the slit in her neck. Other than that, it was as if the little girl was sleeping.

Even as he stumbled over to her pen, his mind told him that it had been done with a razor. He started to reach down and pick up the child, but again his mind informed him that it was a useless action; the baby was dead. Tears blinded him as he staggered around the pen.

Then he saw Mary. She was tied to the end of the marble coffee table. Her throat was cut, too, and she had cuts across her face as if she had tried to fight until the end. But the dead children lying around the room showed how useless it had been. His three-year-old girl was lying close to her mother, only her throat was not cut. The madman had deviated. Instead of the razor, he had strangled the little girl with her own pigtails.

Sam dropped on his knees beside the three-year-old, praying that there still might be life in the small body. His brain screamed over and over again, *Who could be responsible for such a monstrous act?* This wasn't the work of a sane mind. Whoever had committed these insane acts had more than just enjoyed them. He must have received a certain macabre fascination from such grotesque butchery. To be able to kill an adult was one thing; to kill children was another. But to be able to butcher a baby was yet another kind of murdering beast, one who needed to be destroyed at once.

For the moment though, Sam was too stricken even to think of revenge. He wanted to make whoever did this pay, but his mind was too shocked. Could this be some kind of payback for the killing Kingfisher had ordered? It was hard for him to reason that out. He thought he was dealing with men, and even though he knew they were violent men, it had never occurred to him that they were insane, and that was the only explanation he could come up with for whoever had done this gruesome work.

Then suddenly he heard it. It was low at first, but as he listened it grew. The low laughter began almost below the range of his hearing, then it picked up until he could pinpoint the source. He turned toward the sound. He hadn't tried to visualize what the person might have looked like, but now as he turned and saw the bloody human apparition standing behind the full-length window curtains, he knew at once that this debased human was responsible for the destruction of everything he loved in this life. As he stared at the human riffraff, an almost imperceptible hatred increased inside his brain until it was a full-blown desire to destroy this thing.

The sound that came from the man's mouth didn't even seem human; he was enjoying every moment of this. He loved the sight of the grief that had overcome the big heavyset man. It seemed to bring him joy to watch the expressions that flashed across Sam's face.

Sam wanted to kill and destroy, and yet he also

wanted to know. "Why, man? Why the kids?" he asked as he moved slowly across the room, unaware that he had even taken a step. The same question kept coming from him as he stalked the grinning Creeper, who watched him approach with a twisted smile on his face.

The enveloping blackness that invaded Sam's mind stopped him from thinking, or even reasoning. All he could do was move as if he were some kind of automaton—a machine with but one thought. There could be no other reason for him to continue to exist. To destroy, that was the only thought in his mind now. He had to destroy this creature that had so destroyed his life. Whatever else he had to do in life was gone from his thoughts. There wasn't anything left for him to do. His hands turned into huge claws. He didn't make a fist, but held his hands out and continued to move slowly toward the man across the living room. He didn't even notice the thirty-eight automatic with the long silencer that the man now held out in front of him.

The blood on the man's clothes only helped to drive Sam mad. The nearer he got, the more he could smell the stench of death that was on the man. The blood represented his family, his loved ones. The word still came from him as he neared his goal. "Why, why, why?"

The Creeper took his time and concentrated on the huge man's chest. The first shot didn't even seem to hit Sam as he continued his slow stalking of the murderer. There was no squeamishness about the Creeper though. He only grinned and pulled the trigger again. The silencer took care of all the noise. The second bullet that struck Sam sort of slowed him down, but he continued on after hesitating for a second. The third shot went unheeded, and so did the fourth. Now sweat broke out on the Creeper's forehead as he raised the gun a little higher and pulled the trigger. This shot blew the left eye out of Sam's face. He didn't resemble anything human anymore. But a strength derived from his hatred of what stood in front of him kept him on his feet.

The Creeper started to back up but had nowhere to go. The picture window had him blocked in. The only way out was past the stalking Sam, who continued to move, if ever so slowly, toward the killer. With one shot left in his gun, the Creeper took dead aim. Nothing under the sun could stand up to six well-placed shots. Nothing human, anyway.

Now Sam was less than two feet away. He raised his arms to put his hands around the frail neck that was in front of him. He had forgotten why he even wanted to kill this thing in front of him. He was past that form of thinking. He was moving only through of some inner strength that knew what stood in front of him must be destroyed. He stretched his arms out, but the Creeper wasn't a weak man either. Being evil, he thrived on evil. He was also a brave man, and he was a killer. He was a man who didn't need the strength of other men to give him courage. He feared nothing mortal.

Even as Sam approached, even though his heart

skipped a beat, he kept the sneer on his face and kept complete confidence in his gun. He waited until the outstretched fingers almost touched his face before using his last bullet. This time he aimed right at the center of the forehead. Nothing human could survive a shot at such close range. The bullet tore half of Sam's head off. The man crumpled up as if he was a rag doll at the feet of the Creeper.

9

THE DETROIT POLICE DEPARTMENT was caught completely by surprise. The city seemed to burst wide open in a blood bath. They had been used to murder in the surrounding black ghettos, but now, in the last two weeks, three white gangsters, known to have been big men in the organization, had been found dead. The similarity of some of the murders to those that they had found out in Conant Gardens was too close to ignore. Nobody but an insane person killed with a straight razor, and two of the white gangsters had been found with their throats cut. One of them had been found with his wife dead beside him, and she had been killed the same way. There had to be a tie-in somewhere. At least that was what Captain Davidson believed, and this he passed on to his men at a meeting inside his office.

The afternoon sun blazed through his open window. Benson and Ryan loosened their collars, but Detectives Steward and Nelson didn't notice the heat. Their problem was the tough old captain who didn't want to hear any excuses. There had been too many deaths lately. Something would have to be done or somebody would be replaced, and it could be the captain from the way things were going. The captain paced up and down his office, wearing a groove in the dirty, three-colored rug on the floor. It had been there so long that there was a pale outline of where the captain and his predecessor had paced back and forth. Detectives Benson and Ryan watched him calmly. Suddenly he stopped and sat on the edge of his beaten-up desk.

"I don't care for no excuses," he began. "I've had enough of them to last a lifetime. This shit has got to come to an end. This kind of murdering just won't be tolerated by the newspapers, and when the newspapers start playing up something like this, heads begin to roll." He held his hand up for silence. "Now, I don't want to replace any of you guys, 'cause I know you're doing your best, but I'll have to replace somebody just to prove I'm trying. Now, do you see where I'm at?"

He stared around at the four men, his eyes steel gray points peering out over the large horn-rimmed glasses he wore. "I like my job. I mean to keep it. So if something don't come up soon, some of you guys had better dust off those old blue uniforms you used to wear when you were in the ranks."

Suddenly Captain Davidson snapped his fingers in the direction of Detective Steward. The young, blond detective glanced down at the worn rug. "And you," the captain began again, "I asked you two weeks ago to get in touch with Ryan and Benson here about that first murder, but oh, no, not you. You're too fuckin' smart. What did you tell me? Wasn't no spade behind that hit. It had to be organization crap. It was too big for a spade. Wasn't that your opinion?"

The younger man looked away, not wanting Benson to see his eyes and not wanting the captain to see through him. He still couldn't believe that blacks were behind it, unless it was a big, important black gangster, and there really wasn't but one that big in the city.

Steward glanced over at his partner, Nelson, then spoke what was on his mind. "Captain, it's not but one black man in this city big enough to even think about making a hit on these guys, and that's the one they call the Kingfisher."

The roar the captain let out could be heard throughout the building. "Kingfisher, my ass! He's in the same fuckin' pot that all the big shits uptown are in. Those were his men that got knocked off first. Those happened to be his pushers that got knocked off last week. But I forgot. You're too big of a guy to keep up with the little people that get killed in the ghettos. And since you didn't, let me clue you in. That pusher killed last week was one of the Kingfisher's men."

Steward shrugged, then speculated quietly, "Maybe they got a gang war going on? I mean, who else would even have the names of these big wheels? I just can't picture some small hood down in the ghetto coming up with the information he'd need to reach these guys."

For a minute, as Benson watched, he thought the captain was about to have a heart attack. The man turned red in the face, then he seemed to have trouble breathing. He leaned over the desk, trying to catch his breath, and when he straightened up, sparks flew from his eyes.

"Boy," the captain roared, "I don't give a fuck what you can't picture, do you understand that? I want you and your partner to get off your fuckin' asses and do what I say. When I say get in touch with Ryan and Benson and compare notes, I mean just that."

Nobody bothered to speak. They all just stared at the captain. All of them had seen him in his moods before, but nothing like this. He was really upset, which just went to show them how important it must be for them to solve the spree of crimes.

The last thing Benson wanted was to have to work alongside the two young officers whom he disliked, but it looked as if he wouldn't have any choice in the matter. Things had gone too far; there had to be an end to them.

At the same time that they were having their discussion at police headquarters, another meeting was going on at the penthouse that belonged to Kingfisher.

Kingfisher paced his front room just as the captain paced his tiny office, only the Kingfisher was scared—not frightened from fear of losing a job but frightened for his life. It was getting too close for comfort. He didn't need anybody to spell it out for him. He knew beyond a shadow of a doubt that he was on the death list. He glared at his henchmen as he paced past them.

"I'm telling you guys for the last time," he swore angrily, "that I don't want nobody…, and I mean just that, nobody…, who hasn't been here before to get into this apartment. If somebody tries, I want that man or woman held, searched, and make damn sure they don't have no kind of weapon on them. But when I say don't let nobody back here to these apartments, I mean just that. I don't even want a goddamn fly coming in. You guys want me to write that out for you, or do you understand?"

Kingfisher stared from one face to another, then spoke to a lean man standing near the black grand piano. "Big-Time, what's been happenin' on that matter I sent you to? Did you get in touch with the fuckin' creeps?" Before Big-Time could answer any of the questions, Kingfisher began again. "These punks are the reason behind every fuckin' thing going on. I know it, I feel it here." He placed his hand over his heart. "We didn't have no trouble until this punk Kenyatta comes along talkin' about you can't sell no more drugs in the ghetto. Who the fuck does he think he is?"

Finally Big-Time spoke up. "I been going by this joint they got over on the north end, you know, but the place is damn near deserted. I finally caught a dame there and gave her the message, you know, and she says to check back with her the next day. So when I go there, here the bitch is already waiting for me."

He slowed down, to make sure the Kingfisher was listening, then continued. "Well, the dame asked me right off, as soon as I entered the joint, if you done quit pushing dope inside the city. I hesitated for a minute on that one, King, 'cause I didn't know what to say. But before I could even lie, the broad speaks up again. She says they know fuckin' damn well you ain't, but she says to tell you that Kenyatta says he's taking care of your white friends right now and he'll see to it personally that somebody checks you out 'cause you're the one who's really putting that shit in the ghetto."

Before he finished talking, Big-Time had removed a hankie from his center pocket and wiped his brow. He didn't like the message any better than his boss, and it was obvious that the Kingfisher didn't like it at all.

It was as if somebody had hit the Kingfisher in the stomach with a fist. The man stood in the middle of the floor blowing like a fish out of water. "She said that? The part about knockin' off my white friends?"

As the Kingfisher waited for Big-Time to answer, he stared at the man's face, reading whether or not Big-Time was lying. Then he did something that took all his men by surprise: he turned around and counted them. When he finished, he said, "Let's go. I want to talk to this bitch myself."

Eight men got up to leave. "Who we goin' leave to watch the pad?" Big-Time asked when they reached the door.

The Kingfisher stared around in surprise. "Is this all the help I got?" he asked sharply. "Two of you guys stay. That still leaves seven of us, counting myself."

It was left up to Big-Time to appoint two men to stay and watch the place. "Make sure," he ordered sharply, more for his boss' benefit than for the men, "to check on every fuckin' thing that comes near the place. We won't be gone but a short time."

"Should we take both cars?" Big-Time inquired as they reached the downstairs floor. The elevator deposited them in the plush lobby. As they got out, one of Kingfisher's men stuck a key into the lock of the elevator so that nobody would use it until they came back. If the apartment caught on fire, the few people up there would have to use the escape route, taking the stairway, which was closed by a heavy iron door. Other than that, there was no way into the penthouse.

Before the group of men left the plush lobby, a young bellboy made his way to the pay phone. He dialed quickly and spoke quietly into the telephone. He hung up and went back to his work.

"Just bring around the Caddy," Kingfisher ordered before leaving the lobby. With one hand, Big-Time made a sign to the chauffeur, who stayed downstairs

for just such an occasion. The man rushed outside so
that, by the time the rest of the party was reaching the
street, the long Cadillac was pulling up in front of the
apartment building.

All three of the cars were kept parked outside under
the supervision of the man who stayed in the lobby.
It was his job to make sure none of the cars were ever
tampered with. He was also one of the drivers.
Generally, they took along two cars. Kingfisher didn't
like to be crowded. But today he didn't seem to mind
the thought of all seven men squeezing into the car.

As the men walked towards the long car, a black
Ford turned the corner swiftly and bore down on the
group of men. It didn't take a man with a lot of imagination to know what was going on. Even as the car
hurled toward them, they could see the windows
rolling down and the snouts of the short-barreled guns
sticking out of the windows.

The Kingfisher let out a high-pitched scream that
would have done a woman justice. Then the tall, tan-
complexioned man began to scramble toward the
waiting car. He had to shove some of his bodyguards
out of the way, but he managed to throw himself
through the front door of the waiting Cadillac before
the Ford reached them. Some of his gunmen, made
out of better stuff, held their ground, pulling guns
from under their coats. But the pistols were no match
for the bursts from the submachine guns as the car
roared past. All the bullets that struck the Cadillac
bounced off because the car was bulletproof. But the
men standing on the sidewalk weren't. They fell as if

someone had cut them down with a mowing machine.

As the Kingfisher huddled down on the floor of his car, he could feel a weight on his back. He glanced up and saw the frightened face of Big-Time.

"They're gone," the driver, Jack, stated as coldly as he could. He glanced over his shoulder at the men lying on the sidewalk, then glanced down at the two big men lying on the floor. He gritted his teeth. "They knocked off at least three of the boys," he said, his voice not revealing the contempt he felt for both of the men who were on the floor. He could understand running for your life, but he had seen them both push men out of the way who were only trying to get their guns out so that they could defend the two cowards who ran so quickly.

"You still want to make that trip?" Big-Time asked from where he lay huddled on the floor.

Jack had to grin when Kingfisher answered sharply, "The only thing I want, nigger, is for you to get your big ass off of me so I can get the hell out of this goddamn car and get back into the apartment. We goin' have to think on this shit a little more deeper."

Kingfisher climbed out of the car, glancing both ways to make sure there was no chance of his getting caught in the open as he made his dash for the doorway. He didn't bother to pay any attention to his men, whose bodies lay sprawled out on the sidewalk. He had only one thought, and that was to get to the protection of his penthouse, which now had become for him a prison.

10

THE DETECTIVES ARRIVED and the Kingfisher was ready for them. His white lawyer, Mr. Booth, was there to answer all the questions for him. He had only to lie back on his couch and nod his head.

Benson stood on the sidelines and watched. So this was the big man he had heard so much about. *The sonofabitch is so scared he's damn near shittin' in his pants*, the detective reflected coldly.

"So, you say," Nelson asked for what seemed like the twentieth time, "that you saw this car come hurdling around the corner and you knew at once it had hit men in it? Now, you don't really expect us to believe this crap that you didn't recognize any of these so-called hit men, do you?"

The Kingfisher just shrugged his shoulders. "I don't give a flying fuck what you believe," he stated harshly. "I done told you what happened, what I saw, now you can take it from there."

Nelson shrugged his shoulders. He wasn't used to black men talking that way to him. "We could take you downtown, you know. Then maybe you'd feel like cooperating with us."

Benson had to glance away to keep the smile from coming to his lips, but he didn't look away fast enough. His partner, Ryan, recognized the look, and hid his own smile. Taking the Kingfisher downtown on some bullshit would be like sticking your head in a lion's mouth to see if he had a toothache.

Ryan walked over to his partner. "What do you think about all this shit?" he asked seriously.

Benson shrugged. "If the guy really knew anything, he'd talk. Three of his boys got knocked off, one was hurt seriously enough to go to the hospital, plus he's scared so bad he's damn near ready to shit on himself every time somebody comes through that door. He'd talk, all right. You can bet on it."

Ryan nodded. "That's the same way I got it figured, but I think he knows something. I don't know what it is, but he's got a damn good idea who's trying to knock him off."

"We'll see," Benson said as he walked over toward the man on the couch. For some reason, he derived a joyous warmth from seeing the fear in the man. This was the bastard who supplied the whole fuckin' city with dope, and yet none of them could touch him. In fact, they had to handle him with kid gloves, or they would have their asses in a sling by the next day.

It was easy to see from the frowns on Nelson's and Steward's faces that they didn't like the idea of the older detective moving in while they were interrogating the gangster.

"When you finish talking with these boys, King, I'd like to have a private little conversation with you if it's possible," Benson inquired quietly.

The Kingfisher didn't waste any time. He just got up off the couch, ignoring the two young detectives who had been talking to him. "Let's step back in my bedroom. Maybe we can find some kind of privacy there," he said after tossing a look at his lawyer.

Benson shook his head. "It's not necessary for him to come along, but if you want him, it's up to you," Benson said softly.

Before opening the door that led into the bedroom, the Kingfisher stopped and stared silently at the officer. He waved his lawyer off. Neither man spoke until after the door was closed. Benson glanced around the well-furnished bedroom. Everything inside it was expensive. The king-sized bed had a deep red bedspread on it and the carpet on the floor was black, mixed with a dark red strain that matched the rest of the room.

"I might as well come straight to the point," Benson began. "I believe you and I both know who's responsible for this shit. I know you don't want any kind of gang war, but this young bastard I'm thinking about wouldn't care one way or the other." It was a shot in the dark for Benson. He didn't know for sure who was behind the killings.

"You're goddamn right," Kingfisher roared. "That fuckin' Kenyatta ain't got enough sense to pour pee out of a boot!"

So there it was, Benson reflected. After all was said and done, it really was Kenyatta behind it all. "How the hell would a guy like Kenyatta go about gettin' the kind of information he'd need to knock off some of these dagos he's hit?" Benson inquired. "I mean, I can understand him gettin' a fix on you but not on some of them white boys."

Kingfisher tossed his hands in the air. "That's the goddamn problem right there. For a minute some of the big guys thought I was responsible for it, but he's made a hit on one guy that I didn't know shit about." Kingfisher fell silent for a minute, then continued. "After the big boys stopped and put their thinking caps on, they realized that it wouldn't make sense for me to be in on this kind of shit. Why? I mean, I'd have everything to lose and nothing to gain." The Kingfisher shook his head. "Naw, they realize it couldn't be me. I've told them everything I know about this creep, too."

As the Kingfisher talked, Benson realized that the man was trying to sell the idea to himself that the big boys really believed him when he said he didn't have anything to do with it. He must be in the middle of it, Benson reasoned as he watched the bigtime dope pusher try to make sense out of what was happening.

The Kingfisher continued to talk. "Them was black dudes that tried to make that hit on us today; there ain't no doubt about that. I got a good peep at them, even if I can't pick none of them out of a lineup." The man was really talking to himself, trying to figure out what was happening to the world he lived in.

"These punks came out of nowhere, it seemed," he continued. "It was like something out of the roaring twenties. I mean, guys don't go in for this kind of shit no more. It don't pay off. It hurts where it shouldn't, in the pocketbook!"

Benson didn't cut him off. He just let the big man talk. This was the best information he had come up with yet.

"The only problem is where could this punk have gotten the information he's got? If I knew the answer to that one, I'd be able to bust this shit wide open."

All at once Benson changed the conversation. "Where do you suppose a guy like that could come up with the weapons he's gettin', man? I know you could get your hands on a chopper or two, but for the average nigger in the ghetto, buying a submachine gun is like trying to catch a ride to the moon."

Benson watched his face as he asked the question. He knew he was giving out something, but he honestly didn't know where Kenyatta was coming up with the heavy guns.

All at once Kingfisher snapped his fingers. "It ain't many places, I can tell you. Offhand, I couldn't come up with but two or three people...." Suddenly he stopped talking and a light came into his eyes. He

smiled coldly and stood up from the edge of the bed.
"Our interview is over with, copper. I got business to
take care of," he said and opened the bedroom door.

Kingfisher didn't even bother to look back to see
if the detective was following him. He walked straight
over to his lawyer and spoke in a voice that could be
heard all over the room. "How long have we got to
put up with this shit? Can't you get rid of some of
these people? I got business to take care of."

Benson didn't even bother to wait to see how the
little fat lawyer would go about trying to get rid of
the policemen crowding the apartment. He went to his
partner and whispered something in his ear. Both men
left immediately.

Neither man bothered to speak until they reached
the sidewalk. "I think that's the key, Ryan," Benson
said to his partner as they hurried toward the car.
"When I mentioned the gun connect, he almost
jumped out of his skin. It dawned on him then, just
as it did me. The person supplying the information is
the same one Kenyatta gets his guns from. It can't be
any different."

Ryan got behind the steering wheel, listening to his
partner. "I don't know why we didn't see it before.
Now all we got to do is find out who the hell is big
enough to supply the kind of guns Kenyatta is using
and we got our man."

"We already got a damn good idea of who that is,"
Ryan stated as he pulled out into the traffic. He didn't
bother to look at the surprised expression on his partner's face.

"Like hell you say!" Benson exploded. "If we knew that much, we'd have come down on these bastards long before now."

"Well, we can't prove it, but just stop and think. You ain't forgot the day we seen that fat bastard coming out of Kenyatta's place, have you? Well, we checked out the license number and that took us up into a dead end. But don't forget, we also checked out the ownership of the place and found out it was owned by a black man, so whoever fat boy was, I kind of think he was our man."

Ryan fell silent for a minute, then added, "You and I have been doing some piss-poor police work, Ben. We've had this clue and haven't taken advantage of it. Why? Because we weren't sure. But now, we've got to turn up every fuckin' thing."

Ryan watched his partner struggle with the dilemma.

"Okay, Ryan, what now? We didn't see the guy well enough to really recognize him in the mug books." Benson sat up straight and grinned from ear to ear like a kid. "But now that we know the bastard probably handles guns, all we got to do is check out the mug books for bigtime gunrunners, and the first sonofabitch that even resembles that fat bastard will have a hell of a lot of questions to answer."

Ryan picked up speed and cut in and out of the traffic. At last they had something they could put their teeth into. Something a little more solid than a hope or a hunch.

"What about our informers?" Ryan asked as he lit

up a smoke. "You think one of them might be able to come up with something that might also help?"

Benson shook his head. "Naw, it's been too big for them so far, so why even think in that direction. I believe this should be our biggest break. If we get our hands on the man supplying the guns, we got him. I think we better hurry before Kingfisher puts the word out, too. The big boys ain't going to like the idea of someone giving out information on them like this. It's got three of them knocked off already, and no telling how many other names are still on that fuckin' list."

Ryan shook his head in agreement. "I'd sure like to get a look at that list. It would make our work a hell of a lot easier. If we could have gotten the Kingfisher to tell us a little more about who some of his friends are, it would have helped."

"It's easier to get help from hell," Benson answered shortly. "Kingfisher is scared to death, but not that scared."

As they neared the ramp leading to the freeway, a car swerved in front of them, causing Ryan to slam on his brakes. "Damn!" Ryan cursed loudly as both men braced themselves for the sudden stop.

"That's one damn good theory, Ben, about that list. It makes sense, all right. In fact, it makes more sense than anything we've come up with yet."

Benson accepted the compliment quietly. He hoped that he was on the right path. Too many people had been killed.

Ryan cut into his thoughts sharply, bringing him back to reality. "Even with the death of the

Kingfisher's right-hand man, we have to come to the conclusion that it ties in with the murders downtown." Before Benson could add his little bit, Ryan continued, speaking in that soft voice he used whenever he was thinking out loud. "The brutal killing of the children doesn't fit in with gangland killing though. Professional killers would never have butchered the children."

"Maybe the guy was trying to force information from the woman and he attempted to influence her by brutalizing the children." Benson made a small gesture with his hands, then dropped them back into his lap. As he continued to speak, his words came slowly, as if it hurt him to speak.

"Something like this, Ryan, tears me up. I've seen a lot of killings, but the way them kids were done up, it makes me sick to my stomach to even think about it."

The traffic on the freeway was moving swiftly so it didn't take but minutes before Ryan reached his exit, the Jefferson Avenue ramp going west. He came off the freeway and made a right-hand turn.

"I was wondering," Benson began, "if we might have gotten better information from the Feds. A guy who sells guns on this scale might be somebody the FBI would be keepin' tabs on."

"Now you mention it!" Ryan roared. "You wait patiently until I get us back to police headquarters, then you drop this bombshell on me!" Even as he spoke, he drove past the garage where he ordinarily would have parked their car.

As they drove through the main part of downtown, Benson grinned to himself. He could tell his partner liked the idea, even though Ryan didn't come out and say it.

The traffic in the heart of town was congested, but Ryan moved in and out rather swiftly. He got a sharp glance from a policeman on a motorcycle as he got the jump on a crowded bus taking off from the red light from the inside lane.

When he reached Michigan Avenue, he had trouble trying to locate a parking spot. "Why don't you just put the bastard in a no-parking zone?" Benson inquired as they circled the block.

"Man," Benson began, "if I knew we were going to have to hitchhike all the way over to the Federal Building from our parking spot, I'd have called the dispatcher and had him send a squad car to drop us off."

"Like hell!" Ryan answered. "It's just another one of your smart ideas coming eight hours too late, that's all."

On the second time around the block, Ryan saw a driver climbing into his car in front of the Federal Building in a no parking zone. Ryan grinned, pulling into the spot as soon as the driver pulled away from the curb.

"I didn't notice any ticket on his car," Ryan stated, backing up smoothly and parking. Benson got out first and waited on the sidewalk for his partner.

Ryan joined him. "I don't give a shit, Ben, what time it is when we finish, but whatever it is, I'm going to find me some place to eat. I ain't never seen a bastard like you. You just don't believe in eating!"

The men joked back and forth as they made their way into the building and caught the elevator up to the fifth floor. They made their inquiries, then showed their badges. A woman led them down the hall to an almost empty suite. There were two women working, one behind a huge typewriter that looked as if it had seen better days, while the other, a tall blonde, was sitting behind a rather dingy looking desk covered with papers. Both women glanced up when the three-some entered. The tall blonde got up from her desk and came to meet them before they could step behind the enclosure. "You gentlemen will have to wait here at the counter while I bring the mug books to you."

Both men shrugged and waited patiently until she returned carrying three large books. "Well, since you fellows seem to be in good hands, I'll depart," the matronly-looking woman who had brought them to the mug files said.

Neither man glanced up from the books they had taken and laid out on the counter. The woman put the third book next to them and returned to her desk.

For the next hour, both men pored over the books until perspiration was running freely from their brows. The woman had come and gone with fresh books so many times that she became irritated when they called to her for more.

After another hour, Ryan snapped his finger down on a mug shot. "I couldn't swear on it, Ben, 'cause all I got was a side view of the bastard, but this could

be him. Those fuckin' double chins of his were kind
of hard to hide."

Benson glanced over his shoulder at the picture,
then almost shoved his partner out of the way. He
stared hard at the mug shot, while his agile mind went
back to that day in front of Kenyatta's place.

The shrill voice of the blonde interrupted his con-
centration. "It's my lunchtime," she stated harshly.
"You men will just have to come back later today if
you don't have what you want now. We close this
department at lunchtime."

Benson continued to study the mug shot in front of
him, both men ignoring the woman standing there tap-
ping her foot.

Benson finally ended his examination of the picture. He said only two words to his partner: "That's
him!"

The statement was brief, but there was no doubt in
Ryan's mind about whether or not his partner was
right or wrong. If Benson said that was their man,
then that was the man they were going to run down.

As the woman reached over and tried to close the
large book, Ryan coldly shoved her hand away. He
read the name under the picture.

"You think we need a picture of the guy?" Ryan
asked as Benson turned away from the counter.

Again his partner was brief and to the point. "Naw,
it ain't necessary. I say we pick the fat punk up now."

"After we eat," Ryan said, and both men laughed
as they started toward the door.

THE SPRAWLING ACREAGE of the farm was shown to its best when the sun was setting behind the wooded area at the end of the riding paths. The few horses that were kept on the farm were out in the small enclosure behind the huge white barn that contained most of the hay and grain fed to the livestock.

As Kenyatta glanced out of the upstairs bedroom window in the main farmhouse, he could see riders coming out of the wooded section and heading for the huge white barn. Scattered along their path were the many smaller cabins that surrounded the main building. As the horseback riders got closer, Kenyatta could make out his right-hand man, Ali, riding tall in the saddle. The man's name left a bitter taste in his mouth. Ali wanted all the rewards that went with big money, but he didn't want to do anything for it.

Kenyatta finished the cigarette he was smoking and glanced around for an ashtray. His mind wandered back to the conversation he had just had on the phone. His gun connect was finished. The fat honkie was scared to death. The man hadn't been able to accept the killings Kenyatta's people had put on the big white dope pushers.

As Kenyatta thought about it, he smiled grimly. What had the man expected when he took their money for the goddamn information? Did he think Kenyatta was paying out that kind of bread just for kicks? Whatever the bastard thought, he had come out and told Kenyatta that the gun connect was finished.

Finished hell, Kenyatta reflected. If that fat bastard thought he was going to get out of it that easy, he had enough sense to make a jackass fly backward. No way, no fuckin' way in the world was Kenyatta going to allow Angelo's fat ass to get away with his money and the knowledge the man possessed. He was the only one who had the slightest idea of who was behind the hits. If he decided to sell that information, he wouldn't have any trouble finding buyers.

Betty opened the bedroom door and came in carrying a small silver tray with two drinks on it. "Here, honey, I thought you might like something cool."

As he took the offered drink, he smiled down at the tall, attractive black woman. There was something about the way she carried herself—the way she held her head high in a lofty manner. There was the mark of nobility about her. Each time she took a step, her long red gown would open up, revealing a beautiful black leg. Her hair was done up in a huge natural, and her ears were adorned with large African earrings.

"I want you to get on the phone and start calling until you reach the Creeper for me. It's very important that I talk to him at once," Kenyatta ordered as he took the drink, then turned away from the beautiful woman. His mind was on other things at the moment, yet if he kept looking at her, he knew he would end up postponing something while he took a quick roll in the hay.

She seemed to read his mind. "I was hopin', daddy, that you might find time to take care of a little bit of your homework. It's been neglected lately, for some reason," she said in a husky voice that sent ripples up and down his spine.

"Naw, baby, it's not enough time right now. I want you to get on that phone and take care of my business for me," he stated again, still with his back to her.

Even though she hadn't put her hands on him, he could feel her presence. It was like an unwanted alien sending out brain waves that he couldn't cut off. The motivating forces were working, and it showed a weakness on his part. To let his woman have that much power over him was something he resented, while at the same time loving her even more for being able to cause him such a specific emotional disturbance. But it was a disturbance that he didn't want at the time because he had other things on his mind.

She took one more glance at her man and went over to the phone. She sat down on the bed with the telephone in her lap, looking at Kenyatta's stiff back. She couldn't understand why at times she felt as if he was fighting against her, not wanting to allow himself the pleasure of really loving her. Possibly, she thought, he was afraid that he might lose some of his power over her if he were to submit to her demanding love.

Betty dialed the number of the Twenty Grand Motel, but that came up a blank. She tried another motel, but this time she stopped and thought about the man she was trying to reach. The Creeper would probably be hiding in an out-of-the-way place, one that didn't have much traffic. Because of the crime he had committed, she figured he would want seclusion. His very soul should cry out for it, she reflected, as she remembered the news flash she had heard telling about the killing of the small children.

She had known at once that the Creeper was behind it. From conversations she had overheard between her man and that monster, she had put the crime at his doorstep. Nobody else in the organization could or would do something that vicious. Even Kenyatta had been shocked when he heard about it. It had been uncalled for. The death of the children was something that none of them wanted.

As she hesitated with the telephone cradled in her lap, it came to her in a flash. The dilapidated Kingsmen Motel, located over on Grand River Avenue near Davison Street, would be a good place for a man to hide. It was also one of the motels on their list of hideouts.

It took a minute to get Information to give her the number of the motel, and then she put through her call. "Hello," she said in that musical voice of hers. "Do you have a Mr. Marcus Gregory staying there? I don't know his room number, but I'm sure he checked in there sometime this week."

She waited a minute, then the desk man answered that he did have such a guest and put through the call. Suddenly a man's heavy voice was on the other end. "Just a minute," she replied, and held the phone out to Kenyatta, making sure she didn't use any name the switchboard operator could remember. It was bad enough making the call from the country. It could easily be traced if there was ever any need. But the Creeper kept his trail covered up so well she seriously doubted if there would ever be any need.

"What is it?" Kenyatta yelled into the receiver, then waited to make sure he had the person he wanted to talk to. "Listen, bro, I got something important for you, so when you pull up from that joint, stop at a pay phone and give me a ring, okay? Make it as soon as possible, 'cause it's important, my man," Kenyatta stated, then hung up the receiver, not bothering to wait to see if he was understood.

The person who didn't understand was the switchboard operator, who had kept his switchboard key open so that he could hear what was said. He was curious about the strange looking man who stayed in room 12. The man had moved like an animal. At first

the operator had been frightened that the man might
stick him up; then his curiosity had just got the best
of him. The man in number 12 looked like a crimi-
nal to him, yet he hadn't done anything wrong. In fact,
he paid his rent ahead of time and didn't bother him
making silly phone calls all day long like some people.

But the police had asked him to listen in on conversations by people who seemed suspicious. The last
time they had raided a room at the motel, they had
asked him to listen in on any calls by some of the
occupants who rented the high-priced rooms. No black
person living honestly could afford those rates anyway. At least not the daily rates. At one time the motel
had been used by affluent dope pushers, until the
police came through and cleaned it out. Now the
police used the switchboard operator to listen in,
mainly on the ones who drove the long, expensive
Cadillacs. It made him mad to see them pull up in the
driveway. He knew that he would never be able to
buy one of the luxurious cars and resented the long-
haired black men who bought them as if they were
small compact cars. Half of the niggers didn't work.
He could tell that after they had stayed for a week or
two, flashing their huge bankrolls every time they paid
their rent.

There were two Cadillacs sitting in the driveway
now, and one of the owners had two white girls with
him, so the white operator knew that this was probably one of the many black pimps who came in and
out. Now all he was waiting for was a chance to catch

them with some white tricks in their room and he would call the vice squad immediately and bust their asses.

As the man who was going under the name of Marcus Gregory walked out of his room, the operator was trying to decide if it was important enough to call his buddy down on the vice squad. The only thing he had to go on was the fact that the caller had asked him to go out and find a pay phone.

He took a glance out the window just as the Creeper went by. One look at the ugly face on the man made up his mind for him. Any nigger who looked like that had to be up to something wrong. Why else would a woman first ask for him, then let a man take the phone, who then only ordered the ugly bastard to go out and find a pay phone? Yes, he reasoned, as he sat before his switchboard, something out of the ordinary was going on—he would be willing to bet his ass on it. The switchboard operator dialed police headquarters. He knew the number by heart.

Kenyatta sat on the bed rubbing the leg of the beautiful woman who was next to him. Betty stretched out on the bed with her arms thrown back over her head. Maybe, just maybe, she wished silently. For some reason, she couldn't get enough of this man. Kenyatta was her very life.

The telephone in their room rang shrilly. "Yeah," Kenyatta roared into the receiver. "Hang that motherfuckin' receiver up downstairs; I got the phone upstairs here!"

"Hey, baby boy, you at a pay phone now?" He wait-

ed for the reply, then continued. "Listen, brother, I got
an important job for you, man. It's very important,
and it's got to be taken care of immediately. Are you
strapped down for business?"

The Creeper patted the gun under his armpit as if
the man he was talking to could see his action. "I'm
ready and willin', bro," he answered sharply.

"Good, then," Kenyatta replied quickly. "I want
you to put a hit on this white sonofabitch Angelo.
Angelo Benita will be the name he's under. The cat
is staying at the Holiday Inn on Woodward in
Highland Park. You know where the place is?" Again,
Kenyatta waited for the Creeper's answer before continuing. "Now, dig this, bro," he said, making sure he
never used the man's nickname because he sensed that
the Creeper didn't like the name. "Okay, now dig this,
boy. The fat honky is staying in room...." He hesitated and dug out a small piece of paper from his
pocket. "In room 204—that's right, 204. Now, he
should be loaded with bread, but if you ain't got the
time after makin' the hit, fuck the bread. Don't even
worry about it, 'cause you ain't going there after the
money. I want this fat-ass bastard dead before the
fuckin' night is over. And listen, bro, I got this hunch
that the motherfucker is about to split."

The Creeper asked a question and Kenyatta listened
patiently before replying. "Yeah, you know him, bro;
it's the same motherfucker we pick the guns up from.
Yeah, well, the bastard has decided not to supply us
with guns anymore, because of them hits you made
on them bigshot honkies uptown. Yeah, it kind of got

to Angelo so he's decided to freeze us out. That's right, bro, the honky don't want any more of our business, so I want his ass loaded up. Yeah, he's the one who sold us the motherfuckin' list; now he's gettin' an attitude because we're takin' care of business."

Kenyatta listened to the Creeper's heavy voice coming back over the wires, then cut him off. "You got enough bread to hold you, haven't you?" he inquired, then added after the man answered, "Good, that's enough cash for you if something should happen. You know, enough so that you can get around until I can get some more bread to you, but there's also the chance that you might catch Angelo on full, but you had better hurry. Like I said, the peckerwood is gettin' ready to run. Yeah, I can smell it, plus the fact that I think he's going to try and sell us out to them dagos.

"Yeah, they'd love to know who's been knockin' their buddies off, but we ain't goin' give the snitch time to sell us down the drain—not if we can reach him in time. Yeah, so baby, you had better get on the case. Each minute we stand here rappin' about it gives the motherfucker that much more time to slide out of the trap we're about to spring on his white ass."

The telephone went dead in his ear and Kenyatta knew his instrument of death was on its way. If Angelo hadn't already run, he would not live to run tomorrow, because Creeper didn't miss. The man loved his work too much. The thought flashed through Kenyatta's mind about the children that the Creeper had knocked off, and he shrugged. It was something he hadn't foreseen. If he had, he would have given the man direct orders to leave the kids alone. They weren't old enough to hurt them, they couldn't identify him because of their age. So the man had killed them out of pleasure, and only pleasure. No one knew that better than Kenyatta.

After setting the telephone back on the bed, he turned to the woman lying next to him. He took her in his arms and kissed her gently, until his desire became stronger and his embrace tighter. He clutched her to him, feeling her passion matching his. He could think only of what he held in his arms. He pushed the red gown off her shoulders revealing her young, hard nipples. He planted a kiss on each one, nibbling slowly and tenderly.

Suddenly the door flew open. Ali stood there grinning down at the half-naked couple. "I heard you were up here in a business conference, and I thought that I'd come up and join the conference informally."

"Well," Kenyatta growled, his anger rising, "you see we're not in conference now, so how about closing the motherfuckin' door? This ain't no fuckin' peepshow for freaks," he added.

"'Scuse me, boss, iff'n I's done wrong," Ali drawled with a put-on accent.

As Kenyatta rolled over in the bed and sat up, he could see the lust in Ali's eyes. The man still stood in the doorway, allowing his eyes to roam over Betty. He couldn't take his eyes off the woman.

"I ain't goin' ask you again to close that motherfuckin' door," Kenyatta stated, the rage in his voice quite apparent.

"Okay, brother, just keep your shirt on," Ali said as he backed out of the door, his eyes still going over the woman's exposed breasts.

Even after the door was closed and the man was gone, the mood between the two people was broken. Kenyatta sat on the edge of the bed, brooding, trying to decide if he should follow Ali downstairs and bring things to a head. There was something building up between the two men. There was something eating at the man, and it wouldn't let go.

"Honey," Betty began, "please don't let it upset you like that. You know what his problem is, daddy. He just can't accept the idea that you're the big fish in the pond and he's only a small one."

For a second he was tempted to go on downstairs, but the feel of her hands on his bare back, her fingers moving slowly but surely, changed his mind. He slumped back down on the king-sized bed and tried to relax, yet the man's leering face kept coming between him and what he was enjoying. Betty worked slowly. He could feel the slight tug on his pants, then they were off. His shorts came next, and then he stretched out and let himself enjoy the sensations his woman was sending his way.

He closed his eyes as he felt something hot and moist gripping his penis, and then he could feel her tongue moving up and down the sides. The sensation was almost unbearable at first. But then he stretched back and really began to enjoy the love his woman was making to him.

12

AS EVENING BEGAN TO FALL outside the motel, Angelo moved swiftly around his room. It had taken a while for him to make up his mind, but now that it was made up, he knew he wanted to get out of the city for a while. He couldn't understand what force was pushing him, but he was used to playing his hunches. Now, a desperate need to get away was upon him.

The desire to flee the city had come quite suddenly. Them crazy niggers was one thought that came flashing back in his mind. He didn't have any fear of what they might do to him, because he couldn't see any reason for them to want to hurt him. He had left that bastard Kenyatta up in the air over the guns, not telling him straight out that it was over with, just leading him on. He tried to make him believe it would be a short period before they started doing business again. But he knew in his mind that they'd never do business again, not as long as he lived. Them niggers didn't have the sense God gave them, killing every fuckin' body in the city. All they were doing was causing a blood bath, killing like mad dogs.

For the thousandth time, he regretted that he had sold that list to Kenyatta. He hadn't had the slightest notion that the nigger would really follow up his big ideas. He couldn't imagine them spades really reaching the men he had put down on the list. Especially those three men whose names he had used just because they had been in the newspapers lately and everybody took them to be top Mafia men. He had known that none of the three had anything to do with dope. Now one of them was dead, and all because he had been pressed for money. If he had known, he could have put a couple of his debtors on the list. That way, he could have really got something out of it.

As he grabbed the last suits out of the closet, he glanced uneasily toward the doorway. What the hell was wrong with him tonight, he wondered. It wasn't like him to be nervous and jittery for no reason at all. He took another quick glance at his watch. He still had two hours to go before his plane left for Florida, so there was no rush. He had his rented car, and now all he had to do was put his few bags in the trunk and get on his way. It didn't take but twenty minutes to get to the airport, so he would still have over an hour and a half to kill. He couldn't see sitting out there all that time waiting for his plane to take off. Yet he still wanted to rush off.

Impatiently he snapped on the television, then tried to force himself to sit still and watch the six o'clock news. The killing of Kingfisher's men was the top story of the hour, and Angelo watched in shocked horror. He knew who had done it at once. The mention of the submachine guns put him right on their case. After that, the newsman gave a quick rundown on what had happened to the family of Mr. Kingfisher's bodyguard. Kingfisher was described as a "real-estate broker" who was being terrorized by someone in the city demanding money or his life.

Angelo cursed as he got up and began pacing. The mention of the atrocious way the bodyguard's children had been killed sent shivers up his spine. Which one of them bastards would have been behind that, he wondered. Since he knew so many of them, he tried to figure out which one of the niggers he knew could have done it. Then one face came into his mind. He pictured the one they called "the Creeper" as he had seen the man the last time, when he had come to pick up some guns. A shiver ran down his back and he decided he would feel much better being out at the airport with people around him. He could go into the bar and get himself juiced up.

Angelo's mind wouldn't allow him to relax, so he started moving the few bags next to the door. As he went back into the bathroom to get his shaving kit, he wondered if he could sell the information to one of the big boys without getting himself involved. If he came out and told them he had supplied the guns to the niggers, they would put two and two together and come up with his name bigger than shit.

By now, they must have realized that someone had a list with quite a few of the big shots' names on it. The big boys were walking around in a daze hoping like hell their names weren't on that list. So it wouldn't do, no matter how he toyed with the idea, to let them know that he knew the niggers responsible for the mass murders. He couldn't afford to sell his knowledge. Those people played pretty damn rough. They wouldn't accept his denial that he didn't know anything about the list. No, they wouldn't believe him, not if he gave them even a hint of what he knew.

Next, he considered the possibility of calling the police and leaving a tip. The idea intrigued him. Something had to be done. A mad dog had been turned loose, and no matter how he thought about it, Angelo felt as if he were responsible.

Angelo came out of the bathroom with his mind made up. He picked up the telephone and made his call. He asked for the homicide division and spoke hurriedly when the detective answered.

"If you want to know who's behind these killings, check out some punks that have an organization on Clay Street. Their leader is called Kenyatta. I know from personal experience that Kenyatta's people are responsible for the killings that happened today. I saw the submachine guns when they put them in their car."

He quickly hung up, then wiped the sweat off his brow. He smiled, feeling as if he had done at least one good turn today. What was it Kenyatta called him—a snitch? Well, Kenyatta, old boy, I guess you can really call me a snitch now. I just hope they bust your black ass as soon as possible.

Down at headquarters, Detective Nelson called his partner, Steward, over and whispered the information in his ear. Both men got up and slipped out of the office. This was the break they needed. Nelson held a small piece of paper in his hand. "The caller even gave me this address. It won't take us long to check it out. He says they keep their guns hid there, too."

Steward glanced over at him. "You think we might meet with more than we can handle? Maybe we should take some kind of help along."

"Fuck that shit!" Nelson exploded. "I don't plan on allowing none of those bastards to steal this shit from under our noses. Hell no, we can check it out ourselves, and if we need any help, call in a black-and-white squad car as a backup. In fact, when we get there, we can call in a couple of squad cars to help us out."

The two detectives grinned at each other and rushed down in the elevator. This was a chance to put a feather in each of their caps—ones they could be proud of. The captain would have to look at them with a little more respect after this, instead of putting all his faith in that black and white team he seemed to favor.

As the two detectives left the elevator downstairs

in the basement garage, they met Detectives Malloy and Andrews of Vice. Nelson and Steward stopped and waited for the other young detectives to reach them. Steward leaned back on his heels and opened his suitcoat, revealing the double-harness shoulder holster he wore. The two big forty-fives made his suit-coat lopsided.

"When the hell did you start working with Wild Bill Hickok, Nelson?" Detective Malloy asked as they came up.

Nelson just smiled, then said, "Jack, you know how Steward is. He thinks two of everything is better than one, but I'd be damned if I'd want to lug all that heavy artillery around. This fuckin' thirty-eight I have to carry gets in the way too damn much as it is."

Steward only chuckled. He didn't give a damn what they thought about him wearing two pistols. He liked the idea of himself in his checkered red-and-white sports coat with the two guns underneath.

Malloy ignored the young detective after that and spoke to Nelson. "I think I might have something for you. It's only a small lead, but it might just click. We got a call from this informant of ours at a motel over on Grand River. Now, I don't know if it will help you or not, or even if it's your man, because we got this call and just ran by there and checked the guy's room out. There wasn't nothing there, but one thing kept ringing in my mind. I heard about this description you got from the paperboy on that family killing out in Conant Gardens." Malloy hesitated, then added, "It might be nothing, but it rang this bell with me, you know, with the kid calling the guy he saw leaving the house a creeper. Well, we got the very same description from the motel owner, you know. The only way he can describe this guy is by calling him a creeper. So, like I said, it might not be anything, but it is funny that both people resorted to the same description. I mean, it's different—you don't run into it every day, so he must be a hard-lookin' fucker whoever he is." Jack gestured with his hands. "But like I said, it might be nothing; then again, it might give you guys a lead. From what I hear, you could sure as hell stand a lead right about now."

Malloy's partner, Andrews, spoke up. "I wanted to find Ryan and let him know about this. He digs like a bulldog, so something like this would be right up his line."

"Goddamn it, Andrews, you don't have to tell Ryan shit," Steward said, letting his coat fall back in place as he stopped posing. "Me and Nelson can check it out as good as Ryan and that spade he works with."

Andrews glanced sharply at Steward. "I don't know how you meant that, Steward, but I'll tell you one thing. Benson, that so-called spade, is one of the best detectives you'll ever meet, and you can lay odds to that."

At that moment, Steward snorted through his nose as if he'd just gotten a smell of something bad. "Each man to his own opinion, Tom, but I have my doubts about Mr. Benson. He don't raise no hell in my view. I don't see him bustin' this case we're all workin' like hell to open. Naw, he's just living off of past cases.

You guys will see one day, if it weren't for the old
boy Ryan, that spade would probably still be in uni-
form someplace."

"Well, whatever you do," Malloy stated harshly,
"don't let Ryan hear you cuttin' his partner up like
that, because you'd have one mad-ass officer on your
tail!"

"I wouldn't blame him, either," Andrews added.
"Benson has saved Ryan's life on more than one occasion, Steward. And Ryan don't forget things like that.
Especially when a guy steps in front of you and takes
a fuckin' slug from a thirty-eight in his own chest so
that you don't get hit."

"That's new shit to me," Nelson said, trying to pull
his partner out of the hot water he was getting into.

"Yeah, it probably is, but the old-timers around here
know about it," Malloy stated coldly. "It was before
you guys' time. Both of you were still in school when
it happened. And Ryan is one guy who will never forget it. He looks on his colored partner as a friend, so
keep that in mind whenever you're talking about
Benson around him. He won't stand for no shit said
about his partner, and when I say he won't stand for
it, I mean just that. It don't take much to set him off,
either." Malloy turned to his partner. "Well, Tom, we
gave these guys enough to make them heroes if they
follow it up right, so let's get on upstairs and finish
our checker game."

Steward laughed. "That's the sweet thing about vice
detail. All you guys have to do is bust some sweet-
ass broads and relax the rest of the time."

"Yeah, you hit it right on the head," Malloy answered sharply. "That's all we have to do. But if I were you," and again he turned to Nelson. "I'd approach this guy with a lot of care. We just left the motel and it looks as if he will be coming back there, but we didn't have any jurisdiction, so we left. So we decided to pass the information on to you guys, who get paid for working on this kind of crap."

"Okay, we really appreciate it," Nelson said as the two men started to walk away. "And we'll check it out. You never can tell; it might just be the key we've been looking for."

"I'll just bet it is," the two vice men heard Steward say dryly as the men went off in pairs.

"You know," Malloy said loud enough for Steward and Nelson to hear, "that fuckin' Steward is a smart-ass bastard. I'd sure in the hell hate to be in Nelson's position and have to work with that smart-ass every day. Jesus Christ, I couldn't wish that on my worst friend, if you know what I mean."

Nelson had to reach out and grab Steward's arm to hold him back. "Don't worry about cracks like that, man. We got more important things on our minds than what some fuckin' frustrated vice squad dick says. Let's get over there and see if we can shed some kind of light on this case, Stew. With both these leads we got, maybe, just maybe one of them might pay off."

"Okay," Steward answered. "I'll say amen to that. But when we get back, I'm going to ask that smart ass just what he meant by that crack, and you can bet on that."

13

THE CREEPER PEERED OUT of his motel room window. The room he had rented at the Holiday Inn was right across from the one that was still occupied by Angelo. From what he could see through the partially open drapes of Angelo's window, he could tell that the man was getting ready to make his run.

Kenyatta hadn't been wrong about that, he reflected as he watched. The bastard is on his way out as quick as he can go, but ain't he got a surprise coming? He ain't going where he's expectin' to go, the Creeper coldly thought as he watched and waited, trying to make up his mind how to do it. He didn't like to make his hits out in the open, but at the rate Angelo

was moving, it looked as if he would have to knock
the sucker off out in the parking lot.

Suddenly out of the corner of his eyes, he noticed
some movement. It was the maid going into an apartment four doors down from the one that Angelo occupied. It came to him at once. The idea was beautiful.
He found himself moving before he had even finished
thinking it through. It would work, he was sure of it.

He ran down the stairway and up the steps into the
other wing. He slowed down as he approached the
open door where the maid was busy making up the
bed. The heavyset black woman had her back turned
to him as he slipped into the room. She must have
sensed his presence because she was turning around
when he chopped down on the back of her neck with
a judo punch. It was a neck-breaking blow, one that
the Creeper knew how to deliver with ease. He was
always surprised whenever he used it and killed with
just the one blow. It made his pride swell to know
that he could take a life with just one simple action.

The dead black woman meant nothing to him. He
had no emotional feelings about killing her other than
a feeling of pride—pride that he could destroy with
just one well-placed blow to the back of the neck. He
owed this prowess to what Kenyatta had taught him.

He reached down and took the key ring from the
woman's body, examining his work and nodding
silently. *The bitch never knew what hit her*. He chuckled, remembering the long hours he had spent listening to Kenyatta, then doing the things that his leader
had instructed him to do. *Yeah*, thought the Creeper,

that's one black man who really knows his shit.

The Creeper moved quietly to the door, took a quick glance outside to make sure the way was clear, and then slipped out, closing the door firmly behind him. It would be a while before anybody found the woman's body; then it would be too late. He would be long gone. The job that was waiting for him was the one he was concerned with, and he only hoped it would go as smoothly as the murder of the maid. If he could kill the fat man with one blow, there would be no noise to give him away. It would be the perfect murder.

He checked the numbers on the key ring until he found the one he wanted. He hesitated outside the door of Angelo's room, listening. He wanted to make sure the man was by himself. He'd hate to bust in and find some cunt lying up on the bed. Quietly he inserted the key in the lock, and removed the pistol from his shoulder holster. He put his shoulder against the door and pushed. He was in the room before the fat man had any idea he was going to have company.

Angelo glanced up sharply as he heard his door open. His jaw dropped in surprise as he saw the tall, baldheaded man step into the room. The big gun in the black man's hand told him it wasn't a friendly visit. Just the sight of the Creeper caused Angelo to feel as if he was about to have a bowel movement.

"What the fuck's going on here?" he managed to say, trying to get up from the edge of the bed. His legs didn't have any strength in them, so he just sat back down.

"Hello, white boy. You didn't think we were goin' let you leave town with all our money, did you?" the Creeper inquired, as his small reddish eyes searched the room, making sure no one else was there. "Naw, man, we couldn't allow no shit like that. So Kenyatta sent me around to collect it. He says you sold him some bullshit information, some shit he can't use. It seems as if every fuckin' body on the list you gave him is dying for some reason or other." The man let out a cold laugh.

The Creeper leaned over towards Angelo, as if he was going to confide in him. "Yeah, Angelo, ol' boy, as much trouble as we've gone through, it would seem that you would know better than to put shit on my main man like that, so here I am. The collector. I've come to pick up the money you came and collected for a list that wasn't worth a shit."

For a brief second, Angelo felt relief. If it wasn't nothing but a heist, it wouldn't be bad. He could always get some more money, even though he hated the idea of parting with what he had. It was what he had planned to use on his trip, but from the looks of the black man in front of him, this was no time to argue over a few thousand.

"So that's how you guys operate. After all the fuckin' guns I've sold you, you turn around and rip me off. You know, you can tell Kenyatta for me that this ends our gun connection. He'll never get another fuckin' thing out of me."

Angelo was just talking now, trying to make himself believe that nothing more than a heist was going on. His mind wouldn't accept any other idea. It couldn't all come to an end like this. Not in a fuckin' motel room, at the hands of a goddamn nigger. No, he couldn't bring himself to face it.

Angelo got up and walked over to his suitcase.

"Now, don't make no sudden moves while you're playin' around there," Creeper warned him sharply as he came around the bed behind him.

Shivers went up and down Angelo's spine at the nearness of the man. "I'm just gettin' the fuckin' money for you. Ain't that what you said you came for?" Angelo snapped, trying to muster up the courage he didn't have. He could hardly stand because his knees were shaking so badly. He pulled out a package of money, wrapped with the amount written across the paper. As he did this, he tried to cover up another package of money that was of the same amount.

"Here, take it; it's five grand there. Just what Kenyatta paid for the list. Tell him for me that I've got a hell of a shipment of guns coming, and I know he'll want them. But before he can get them, he'll have to kick back this bread that you're rippin' me off for. I mean every fuckin' word of it, too," Angelo said, fooling no one but himself, unable to face the fact that he would never leave that room alive.

The small pistol that he had hidden at the bottom of his suitcase stayed right there. He just didn't have the nerve to try for it. At least not while he believed he might be able to talk his way out of the situation.

The Creeper studied him icily. "You know, the way you pulled that package out, I I have a feeling it's not the only money you have there. I mean, I wouldn't be able to sleep nights if I thought I left with only half the money while you still had more."

Angelo turned on him angrily. "Just what the hell is this? A rip-off? You said you came after the five grand that Kenyatta paid for the list!" Angelo found courage in his desperation. The prospect of losing all of his money affected the fat man deeply.

"What do you really think it is, white boy?" Creeper said, as he pulled the razor out of his pocket and advanced towards the frightened man.

It was out in the open now. This man had come to kill him. Angelo stalled for time. "Wait, here, I'll give you all the money, just don't cut me." Angelo wasn't truly a coward. He had come up in the old school with some of the meanest dagos the city had ever produced, but this one black man had made him lose his balls for a minute. Now, faced with certain death, his courage returned. It was the courage of a cornered rat.

"I got ten thousand dollars more here," Angelo said abruptly, hoping he could fool the man who had come to kill him.

"Ten grand more!" the Creeper shouted. That was more money than he had ever seen in his life. Even though he didn't care that much about money, he knew that, if he returned with fifteen thousand dollars, Kenyatta would be pleased as hell. As these thoughts flew through his mind, Creeper made one of the first big mistakes he had made since becoming a professional hit man; he took his eyes off the fat man. Angelo took out the other package of money and tossed it on the bed, then went back to looking in the suitcase as if he was searching for another one.

The bundle of money hit the bed and fell to the floor. The Creeper's eyes followed the package, noticing that it was wrapped like the one he had already stuck in his pocket. There was writing on the wrapping, and as he reached down and picked it up, he could see that the amount was five thousand dollars.

While mentally counting the money, the Creeper believed that the frightened fat man was searching for a third package. With that one, he would have the fifteen grand the man said he had, and then he could get on with cutting the honky's throat.

He was just straightening up from picking up the package when the fat man made his move. Angelo spun around, swinging the suitcase, and as the suitcase struck the Creeper in the chest, the fat man raised the small Derringer he had palmed and fired. The suitcase seemed to have done more damage to the Creeper than the little gun. The two quick shots that struck him in the stomach didn't faze him at all. He raised the thirty-eight in his left hand, dropping the straight razor to the floor.

The sound of the police special going off in the small room was deafening. The first shot caught Angelo high in the chest, slamming him back against the wall. The second shot struck two inches away from the first one.

As Angelo struggled to raise the small pistol, he remembered that it was only a two-shot Derringer. The gun clicked on empty chambers.

As the Creeper turned away from the dying man, he could feel the pain starting to spread in his stomach. He clutched at his guts and staggered around the big bed. He noticed a towel lying on the top of the end table and snatched it up. He stuck it inside his shirt, trying to stop the flow of blood, cursing loudly. "The sonofabitching honky faked me out," he murmured as he started to make his way from the room.

His mind was racing. He knew he would have to get away, and quick. The sounds of his thirty-eight going off had been loud enough to awaken the dead. He staggered to the door and somehow managed to snatch it open. As he stumbled from the room, still clutching the thirty-eight tightly in his fist, he struggled to reach the iron railing and caught his balance. Out of the corner of his eye, he could make out two men rushing up the stairway. His brain warned him that it was the police. He realized at once that he couldn't outrun them. He raised the gun up as the first officer came up the steps.

For some reason he couldn't seem to draw his bead on the man, who stopped and yelled, "Drop it, police!" That was the only warning he got. The second man, who appeared to be a black man, raised his weapon and fired. The shot picked him up and threw him backwards. He could feel himself falling, and then the concrete struck him in the back.

"Goddamn it, Ben, I wanted to take him alive." The Creeper heard the words coming as if they were from a great distance. Even then he attempted to raise the gun in his hand. But someone kicked the weapon away.

"Yeah, I know; you wanted him alive bad enough to get shot up for it," Benson said sharply, bending over the Creeper's body. "Looks as if somebody else shot him before I hit him," Benson said after making a quick examination.

Ryan took a quick look inside the motel room. "There's another one inside. I better check and find out if he's cashed in his chips yet." He went inside and leaned down over Angelo.

When Angelo tried to speak, blood came gushing out of his mouth. "I'm on my last ride," he managed to say.

"Who's responsible for this?," Ryan asked Angelo sharply, almost pulling the wounded man up to his feet. He bent down and listened as the man tried to speak. "It's that fuckin' Kenyatta. He's gone mad. I shouldn't have ever sold him that list." Again blood came out of the man's mouth. "All my fault.... I sold him the fuckin' list."

"Where can we find Kenyatta? Where, Angelo, where the hell does he hide out?"

At first Ryan thought the question would go unanswered, but somehow the man managed to raise up on his elbow and speak. "Farm, he's got a farm," but as he tried to give the information, he coughed up the last life in his body. Dark blood ran down his chin.

Ryan didn't need a doctor to tell him that the man was dead.

14

DETECTIVES NELSON and Steward decided to give up the stakeout on the motel. After all, they were sitting around waiting for a man they weren't sure they wanted. When the call came over their two-way radio about the shoot-out at the Holiday Inn, they decided to drive over and check it out. Upon their arrival, the first thing they noticed was the car belonging to Detectives Benson and Ryan.

"We should have known these bastards would be up on the fuckin' shoot-out," Nelson growled as he tried to find a place to park.

Had the two detectives not been so busy cursing out their rivals, they would have noticed the two well-dressed black couples making their way out of the crowd of curious onlookers around the courtyard. What was so peculiar about the two couples was that both men, and one of the women, had their hair completely shaved off. Their heads shone with some kind of lotion beneath the bright neon lights.

The two couples hurried away from the crowd toward a parked car near the parking lot of the Holiday Inn. Neither detective noticed because they were too busy with their petty jealousy.

"These fuckin' guys get all the breaks," Detective Steward said before getting out of the car.

As Detectives Nelson and Steward bellyached to each other, the four members of Kenyatta's organization made their way to their car. It was of the utmost importance that they reach Kenyatta at once to let him know what had just happened at the motel. Their orders had been to check into the Holiday Inn to make sure Kenyatta's orders had been carried out. Only one of them had known what the leader's orders had been. But with the killing of their best hit man, whom all of them recognized on sight, they knew something had gone wrong.

They had stayed long enough to find out just what had happened inside the room. They knew the white man and the black maid had been killed. This they had witnessed themselves. Eddie-Bee had been at the window and had seen the Creeper when he slipped in the open doorway behind the maid's back. And afterwards, while the Creeper was busy elsewhere, Jug had run over to check it out, bringing back the news that the elderly black woman was, indeed, dead.

Jug settled his lean, angular body into the driver's seat of the rented black Chevy and started the motor. Eddie-Bee got into the backseat with his woman. Each man had brought his girlfriend along to make it look legitimate when they checked into the double suite at the motel.

For Eddie-Bee, who had been in on the holdup of the stamp place, this was a cakewalk. He only wished all his assignments were this easy.

"As soon as you see a pay phone, pull over," Eddie-Bee ordered loudly from the rear of the car.

"Hey, man," Jug yelled back, resenting the idea of the man telling him what was obvious. "When I need some advice I'll ask for it, okay? But telling me what any fool would realize is something I don't appreciate."

From the tone of Jug's voice, Eddie-Bee realized he had overstepped the bounds in trying to be helpful. "Okay, baby, don't get no attitude," Eddie-Bee said quickly. "I was just trying to be helpful, that's all."

"There's a pay phone over on your right," Jug's girlfriend Almeta stated. She was rather tall, and completely bald, just like her man. If it wasn't for her huge chest, people would take her for a man at first glance.

After a quick look, Jug swung to the curb next to the phone booth. Almeta had trouble beating Eddie-Bee out of the car because he tried to push the seat up so that he could get out first.

"Slow down, man," Jug cautioned. "It don't make no difference which one of us makes the report. We're all together on this job, so just be cool. You ain't goin' gain nothing or lose nothing by being the one to report it to Kenyatta."

Eddie-Bee sat back in his seat. He wished he had been the one to break the news to Kenyatta, but it had been impossible to get out of the car before Almeta.

After one more cold glance at the man in the rear, Jug shook his head in disgust. "I don't know how you put up with such a nigger, Penny," he stated, looking at Eddie-Bee's woman in his rearview mirror.

Penny just shook her head. "You know it's a man shortage in the streets, Jug, so sometimes a girl has to take what comes along." She laughed to take the sting out of her words.

It didn't take but two or three minutes before Almeta rejoined them in the car. "I got in touch with Kenyatta," she stated breathlessly, as if she had just run a mile, "but Ali answered the phone, and do you know that nigger didn't want to put Kenyatta on the line until I told him what it was about. I mean, he just wouldn't call Kenyatta."

She sounded dumbfounded about the situation but continued. "I know he'd like to take Kenyatta's place, but if he was in charge, I'd quit. Just like that, I'd give up the organization, because he's too much for me. He thinks he's too pretty, first of all. Then he believes he's the only person with any sense. Ain't nobody else got no brains but him, if you listen to him. That's the impression he gives me anyway."

"Shit!" Penny sighed loudly. "I think Ali's one fine black nigger, if you ask me."

"It's a good thing didn't nobody ask you then," Eddie-Bee stated coldly, his anger showing in his voice.

"Aw, honey," Penny said, rubbing his jaw, "ain't no reason you gettin' jealous, 'cause as long as you're around, there ain't no room in my heart for no other man."

"I'll bet," Jug said under his breath so that the rest of them didn't hear. "What did Kenyatta say after you gave him the news?" he inquired loudly.

"Oh...," Almeta moaned, surprised by the simple question. "He wants us to get out to the farm at once. It took him by surprise that the Creeper got himself killed, but not me. I'm glad the dirty, murdering sonofabitch is dead." She spoke with more venom than she realized. "I couldn't stand the sight of him as it was. Then after those murders he did, shit. Well, all I got to say is I hope don't nobody else join our organization like him. I ain't never seen no man like him before, and I hope I don't live long enough to meet another one."

"I'll say amen to that," Penny replied quickly. "He was a murdering bastard at that. There was no reason for him to kill that maid. Did you tell Kenyatta about him killin' the maid?"

"No, there was no time for that," Almeta replied softly. "As soon as I told him about Creeper gettin' cut down as he came out of the motel room, he wanted to know if the Creeper took care of his homework, to which I replied yes. I was sure of that. They carried the fat man out on a long stretcher with his face covered up. I didn't see his face, like I told him, but from the shape on that stretcher, it had to be fat boy. Couldn't nobody else have a belly stickin' up in the air like that."

Suddenly Jug made a sharp turn off Woodward. "I want to hit the freeway as soon as possible. I think we had better get out to the farm fast. Things might start jumping around town, and everybody will have to go in hiding." Jug meticulously picked his way through the evening traffic.

Almeta rolled her window up. "Damn if it ain't gettin' chilly out," she stated. "I don't know if it's all that safe at the farm. What do you think about it, Jug?"

"Well, I'm on my way out there, whether or not it's safe. We've made plans in case this kind of thing happened. If it comes down to it, we just go into what Kenyatta calls 'Operation Break-Out.' We all know about it, so now will be the time to put it into action—if it comes to that."

His words brought silence to the people in the car. Each one was filled with his or her own thoughts. No one really wanted to go through with the so-called 'Operation Break-Out,' but it had been planned, and everybody knew what their roles in it would be.

While the car with its four occupants fled towards the outskirts of town, two detectives back at the motel were trying to wrap up the case.

Benson walked into the room, feeling the two heavy packages of money he had removed from the

dead man's body in his pockets. He was still undecided on whether or not to give one of them to his
partner. "Did you get anything out of your man before
he died?" he inquired of Ryan.

Ryan looked up tiredly. "I don't know, Ben. He
mentioned something about a farm, but that was about
it. What about your man out there? Did he have anything to say before he passed on to the hell waiting
for him?"

Benson managed to grin. "Yeah, he managed to
gain enough strength to spit in my face before he
kicked off," Benson answered truthfully. "That bastard was mean through and through. I don't think there
was a kind streak in him anywhere."

"I'm inclined to believe you there. But it looks like
he made a mistake about our boy Angelo here. It turns
out Angelo was a little bit rougher than he had
thought." Ryan held up the little pee-shooter Angelo
had used to punch two holes in the Creeper's belly.
"He hit his man, didn't he?"

"Yeah," Benson answered, "it's like I told you. It
wasn't just my shot that put him away. When we saw
him reeling, it was from them two shots he had in his
gut."

As the other policemen began pouring into the
small motel room, Ryan asked his partner if he had
found anything of value on the dead man.

Benson shrugged. "It depends on what you call
value." He nodded his head towards the toilet. "Let's
step in the men's room for a minute. I got something
I'd like to show you."

Ryan followed his partner into the bathroom. Neither man spoke until Benson closed the door and leaned against it.

"Well, what is it? Did the guy give us a lead?" Ryan asked impatiently.

"Naw, it ain't no fuckin' lead," Benson replied, then removed one bundle of money from his pocket and tossed it towards his partner. "He did have that on him, so I wondered if you and I could use it, or should we turn it in for evidence that will never be used."

For the next five minutes Benson watched his friend and partner change expressions. "Not me, Ben. What do you want to do about it?"

Without realizing it, Benson fingered the other bank notes in his pocket. He knew what he was going to do. This time he would come out with something if the captain should ever make good on one of his many threats to remove him from his position. Whatever Ryan decided to do with the bundle of money he had tossed to him was all right with him, but the one in his pocket was going to stay there.

"No, Ryan, it's not my decision. If I was going to keep it for myself, you would never have known. But I wanted you up on it. It's a nice piece of money, and nobody will miss it. If you want to, we can split it up between us. If not, turn it in, but don't ask me to make the decision. That way, if you have guilty thoughts later on, I don't want you blaming me. I'll go along with you either way. I could use the money, and so could you, but it's your baby. Make up your own mind."

"Goddamn it, Ben, why the hell do you do these kind of things to me? Ain't I got enough problems worrying about this fuckin' case without you tossin' temptation in front of me like this?"

"We ain't gettin' no younger, Ryan. If something bad should happen to either one of us, this would go a long way towards helpin' the few people in the world who mean anything to us."

It took a second, but finally a sheepish grin broke out over Ryan's face. "Well, I guess it ain't like being on the take. It must have been the money the bastard got for trying to make the hit on Angelo."

The two men stared at each other, and finally Benson broke the silence. "Then I take it, you'll go along with holding back this small sum for ourselves?"

Ryan shook his head undecidedly. "I just don't know yet, Ben. Let's sit on it for a while, okay?"

Their eyes met, and then Ryan glanced away, but not before Benson could read the greed there. Ryan wanted the money, but just didn't know how to go about keeping it. His conscience would bother him for a while, but Benson was sure he would get over it.

A sudden commotion in the outer room brought both detectives rushing out. To their astonishment they foundNelson and Steward there, trying to take charge.

"Hold on, boys," Ryan said harshly. "I've already given these men their orders, so don't interfere. This is our little problem, so you guys just take a backseat."

As the detectives dickered among themselves, Kenyatta was busy making calls from his farm. He was also making one final decision—one that involved the Kingfisher.

"Listen, Jerry, I've tried every way possible to get this hit made without using you. But I put you in the position you're in, just in case something like this came up. Well, it's up. There is no other way out of this. Either you make the hit on the Kingfisher or the bastard gets away."

There was silence on the other end of the line. For a minute Kenyatta wondered if the man had hung up. But then he spoke in a low voice. "Well, what do you want me to do?"

"Do?" Kenyatta roared. "Why, I want you to assassinate the bastard. Shoot the motherfucker down like the dog that he is. If you do this, Jerry, you'll save hundreds of black lives—hundreds!" Kenyatta did not add that the man would also be giving up his own life when he followed through with the order.

"How?" Jerry asked.

To Kenyatta the question was too simple. It showed that the man wasn't using his head. It might benefit Jerry to act like he was a robot sometimes, but Kenyatta knew that this job required a man to use his brain.

"How!" Kenyatta repeated loudly. "Man, you're not even trying to think, Jerry. I got you that job there in the apartment building because you were one of my best trained men, and most faithful. Remember your baby sister dying from the overdose?"

Kenyatta knew that should be enough to convince him, but he continued anyway. "Well, I can damn near prove the dope came from the Kingfisher, but all that shit ain't necessary. Either you're going to do it or not. If you are, this is all you have to do. When the Kingfisher and his men come back downstairs, you get as close as possible and cut loose with that thirty-eight I gave you. As good a shot as you are, it shouldn't take but one shitty-ass shot, but I want you to be sure to hit him twice. You got that, Jerry? When he comes out through the lobby, you're to make your hit!"

This time there was a long silence before the man finally spoke. "I understand, Kenyatta. This is what I've been trained for, so I'll do it. I'm as dedicated as anybody else in the organization."

"Good. Just make sure you don't miss, Jerry. Make damn sure you don't miss. And don't forget, put two slugs in his dope-selling ass. You hear me? One for your sister and one for the rest of the kids who have died from the poison his men have been selling in our neighborhoods."

Kenyatta waited until the man answered affirmatively. "Okay, then. When you hang up, go get your piece. You ain't got no time to waste. We want this bastard dead before he receives the new shipment of dope coming in. We can't cut the shipment off, but if we hit the Kingfisher, he won't be able to distribute that fuckin' poison!"

After hanging up the telephone, Jerry moved as if he was under some kind of spell. First, he went down

to the locker room and opened up his locker. From it
he took out the still-new thirty-eight automatic. The
gun shined from constant polishing. It had never been
fired. He picked out six bullets from a full box, then
put the rest back into his locker. He laid the gun and
bullets out on the bench that he used when changing
in and out of his work clothes.

After he finished putting on his fresh bellboy uni-
form, Jerry had trouble figuring out where to put the
gun. If he stuck it in his belt, it would make a bulge.
He might be able to conceal it under his arm, but he
didn't have a shoulder holster to make it stay in place.
He sat down on the bench for ten minutes trying to
figure out what to do with the gun.

Suddenly he got an idea. He stood up, put the gun
in his belt, next to the small part of his back, then
pulled his coat down over it. It didn't seem to bulge
too much, and if he kept his back turned, nobody
would notice it anyway. At last Jerry was ready. At
no time had he doubted that he would go through with
his assignment. This was what he had been trained
for, his purpose in being here. He made his way back
up the steps with swiftness and certainty. He was now
a dedicated man with a mission.

It happened sooner than he hoped for. Jerry hadn't
been in the lobby more than forty minutes when the
private elevator that handled only the Kingfisher's
penthouse began to come down. Jerry watched the dial
as it moved lower and lower.

Kingfisher stood in the elevator smiling. He had
heard the news on the television and had watched the

film clips of the bodies being removed from the Holiday Inn. He knew the identity of the man the Creeper had gunned down. Just a short time earlier he had put through a call and had told some big men his idea about somebody selling guns to the blacks in the ghetto, and the name "Angelo" had been one of those mentioned as the possible seller. As soon as this had been brought to the big men's attention, they had made the logical connections. Whoever supplied the guns was more than likely the same man who supplied the blacks with the list of people bringing dope into the city.

Now that the gun runner was dead, it wouldn't take long before the men who had bought the guns would be out searching for another connect, thus exposing themselves. When they did, they would be taken care of. To celebrate, the Kingfisher was taking everybody in his place out on the town.

Vickie, the Kingfisher's special woman, smiled broadly for the first time in what seemed like months, fussing over which expensive gown she should wear—the gold one or the navy blue one that looked good with the string of pearls Kingfisher had bought for her. She decided to wear the low-cut gold gown. It revealed more in the front and back.

She dressed with care. It had been so long, so goddamn long since they had been anywhere. She could hear Kingfisher singing in the bedroom as he dressed. What a time they would have tonight. It seemed as if they had been living under the shadow of fear for so

long that they had been tempted to run off. Just pack
a few of the expensive things Kingfisher had bought
for her and leave town. The news on the television
meant that was all over now and everybody seemed
happy.

"Let's go," the Kingfisher called out happily. It had
been quite a while since anyone had seen him in such
a good mood.

Vickie rushed out of the bedroom and joined the
rest of the party at the elevator. They waited while
one of the bodyguards used his key to open up the
doors. Then the small party of five people walked in.
Besides Vickie and Kingfisher, there were three bodyguards going along. It was quite a cutback from the
time when the Kingfisher wouldn't go out with fewer
than six bodyguards.

As soon as the elevator door opened at the ground
floor, the bodyguards got out. They didn't notice anything out of the ordinary. The bellboy standing near
the door was the same one they had seen many times
before.

As Kingfisher stepped from the elevator with a big
smile on his face, he noticed the youthful bellboy start
towards them.

Jerry reached behind his back, and the next thing
Kingfisher saw was the long barrel of a thirty-eight
automatic pointed directly at him. His heart froze. The
warning yell he gave to his bodyguards was too late.
He attempted to duck behind his woman. Vickie let
out a scream of fear as she felt Kingfisher trying to
use her for a shield. But the young gunman wouldn't

be denied. He pushed the gun in Kingfisher's face and pulled the trigger.

The roar of the thirty-eight was deafening, as were the answering shots that cut the young boy down in his tracks.

The Kingfisher's body had slid down the wall. The bellboy had been struck from two different sides. Kingfisher's bodyguards were not slow; they had just been taken completely by surprise. The two shots fired by the bellboy had struck the Kingfisher high in the neck. He had been dead before he reached the luxurious carpet. Kingfisher didn't live long enough to know that his bodyguards had done their job, at least avenging him, if not managing to protect him.

15

AS THE POLICE LEFT Kenyatta's club on the north side of Detroit and headed towards the farm in the country, some of the people on the farm were making hurried efforts to leave. As soon as the club had been raided, Kenyatta had been called and duly informed. The few members inside the club hadn't stood up too long before giving out the information on Kenyatta's whereabouts, but that was something Kenyatta had expected.

Kenyatta was well armed when he left the farm, taking four men with him. Each of the men took his woman along in one of the two cars—Jug and his girlfriend, Almeta; Eddie-Bee with his lady, and Red and

Arlene, the woman who had gotten rid of the guns for them after the holdup.

Kenyatta and Betty, with over thirty thousand dollars in a black briefcase between them, rode with Zeke and his black queen. Each couple was armed to the teeth, men and women alike, as they pulled out of the farmyard.

The rest of the people watched them go, not knowing when their leader would return. Ali stood at the front door scratching his chin. He had been left in charge, and that was all that mattered to him, but he could feel something wrong. He couldn't know that his rule would last only a few hours.

Ali didn't have the knowledge that Kenyatta possessed. He was uninformed about the raid on the city clubhouse, and he didn't know that an army of police were on their way to the farm at that very moment.

When Kenyatta and his group reached the airport, they parked the cars in a no-standing zone, abandoning them. None of them had any thoughts of returning that way. It was time to get out. It was a well-thought-out plan of escape. Now was the time to put it to use.

Everybody followed Kenyatta into the airport. As he bypassed the ticket windows, he turned and joked with his followers. "Now that sure in the hell would be a waste of money, wouldn't it?" he said as he shifted the heavy black bag around in his left hand.

All of the women carried big, heavy shoulderbags. Each couple carried a certain amount of cash on them, in case they ran into more trouble than they could handle and had to split up, but none of them had as much as Kenyatta carried.

They waited about ten minutes until people started boarding a nonstop flight to California, then Kenyatta led his small group toward the loading ramp. The airport was set up in such a way that they didn't check for weapons until a person was going onto the ramp that led into the plane. Here a few guards stood around looking bored, watching the metal detector to see if anyone was possibly carrying a weapon.

When Kenyatta's group reached them, there was no suspicion because the group was well-dressed and smiling. They came up to the ramp as if they had tickets, then all at once hell broke loose. Kenyatta pulled out an automatic. He waved it at the guards as his people came rushing up beside him. With a wave of his hand, he sent Red rushing up the ramp.

The sight of the black men trying to commandeer the plane sent the guards into action. As Red came rushing up, one tried to reach out and stop him with his arms, while another took a step back and pulled out his gun. Neither man found success. The first one took a bullet from Red's gun right in the face. Blood flew everywhere as the white guard crumpled to the floor. There was a red gash where his face had been.

As the second guard came out with his gun, Red's woman, who was just a step behind him, shot from the hip and took the guard by surprise. Her first shot hit him high in the chest, spinning him around. The second shot took the back of his head off. The couple ran past, not bothering to see the object of their handiwork fall to the floor.

"Everybody stay still," Kenyatta ordered loudly, "and won't nobody get hurt." As he spoke, a guard on Kenyatta's blind side made his move. As soon as the man reached for his weapon, Betty stepped around her man and raised the sawed-off shotgun she carried in her bag. The gun was cut off so that it was almost as short as a pistol. She gave the man both barrels. The sight of what the shotgun did froze the other men in fear. There was no doubt in their minds now that the blacks meant business.

Kenyatta backed up the ramp, using the girl who had been at the checkpoint as his shield. He stopped and waved Betty and the rest of his crowd past. They rushed up the ramp towards Red, who had the steward shaking from fear under the sight of his gun.

Kenyatta's measured words roared out over the airport. "You honkies had better pay heed, or we'll kill everything white on the plane." A dark flush stained his lean and sallow cheeks as rage glittered in his cold black eyes.

The sight of the terrified white girl in the tall black man's arms made the guards hesitate. There was no doubt that he would kill her. The guards held their weapons in check and allowed Kenyatta to make his way on up the ramp.

Eddie-Bee stood at the top of the ramp waiting for him, while he pointed two thirty-eight short-nosed police specials at the white men at the bottom of the ramp.

"That's right!" Kenyatta roared as he backed into

the plane, followed by Eddie-Bee. "If you don't want any dead passengers or stewards, keep your hands off them motherfuckin' guns." His voice carried all the way through the plane, causing a near panic among the passengers.

The members of his gang had already taken complete command of the plane. The pilot of the plane was well aware of the fact that his plane had been commandeered by a bunch of black gunmen. He reached the tower by radio and asked for information on what to do.

"Follow their orders. Don't endanger any of the passengers!" the voice from the tower replied. "The people who have taken control of your plane are murderers. They have just killed at least four people in the terminal, so be careful."

The co-pilot glanced over at the captain; their eyes locked for a quiet moment, but that was broken by the entry of Zeke. The tall black man stood in the cockpit with a cocked gun in his hand. He aimed it at the back of the co-pilot's head. "There won't be any trouble if you don't give us any," the black man stated harshly.

From the way the man spoke, the pilot knew he meant business. "Where to?" the pilot asked softly.

"When we get off the ground, I'll let you know," Zeke replied, then smiled. It had gone easier than Kenyatta had said it would. "Wherever we go," he said offhandedly, "you can bet it will be a black country. Yes indeed," Zeke said, speaking more to himself than the white pilots. "It's goin' sure nuff be black!"

Donald Goines
SPECIAL PREVIEW

CRY
REVENGE

This excerpt from Cry Revenge *will introduce you to Curtis Carson, a young man who doesn't really mean to rip off the Chicanos in his backyard crap games; he just rolls the dice better. But the Chicanos don't see it that way, and when one of their brothers is brutally slaughtered in a barroom shootout because of Curtis' dealings with heroin pusher Fat George, the Mexicans cry revenge on Curtis, leaving his brother with a wrecked body that will forever prevent him from being the basketball star he had always dreamed of being. Curtis swears vengeance, and the streets run red with Black–Chicano warfare!*

/

IN THE BACKYARD of the white frame house was sand. Brown, light sand that blew in from the distant desert. New Mexico was more desert than anything else, yet it still possessed a beauty that would be hard to find elsewhere.

Curtis Carson stood up and put his hands on his hips as he shook out the kinks in his back. He stared down at the dice that his friend Dan Lewis shook.

"Seven!" Dan yelled as he rolled the dice out. When eight showed, he snatched them back up quickly. "Seven," he yelled again, this time taking his time and trying to roll the dice gently on the sand. Again the dice came up with eight.

"These mothafuckers ain't got nothin' on them but eights," Dan cursed loudly. Then he shook the dice slowly, holding them back near his ear. He grinned up at Curtis, who picked up the money he had made after jumping eight. "Now," Dan yelled, "I want to see some fuckin' sevens on these mothahuppas."

The two Mexican men kneeling in the dirt watched Dan closely as he shook the dice. The stouter of the two tossed his money down beside Dan's. "Okay, momma," he said, drawing the words out, "you're faded."

Dan stared down at the ten-dollar bill lying in the dirt. He grinned up at the men, revealing good teeth that needed some cleaning. "Now that's the way I like to get my money on, with no problems." He took his time, then quickly released the dice. The dice hit the dirt and began to spin around like small tops.

Before the dice could stop spinning, the Mexican who had faded the money reached over and snatched the dice up from the dirt. "Goddamn, Dannie, how many times we got to go over it! Ain't goin' be no spinning the dice in the sand!"

"The sonofabitch," the other Mexican said, loud enough for all the men in the game to hear. "The gringo bastard must think we are the fools, huh?"

"Hey, amigo," Curtis said smoothly, "sometimes people forget, you know. Ain't nobody been hurt, the dice were caught, so let's not get nasty about it, okay?" His voice had remained low, but there was no doubt about the authority in it. The tall black was used to giving orders.

The slim Mexican who had spoken glanced up from his kneeling position. "Hey, my man, how many times do we have to pull this dude's coat about tryin' to shoot that shot on us, huh?"

Curtis shrugged his wide shoulders. "These things happen, Pedro, you're hip to it. The guy is used to firin' the craps that way, so all at once we want him to change his style of shootin' 'cause you guys say he's gettin' slick. So the guy tries and changes his style of shootin', but at times he forgets, you know, and goes back to firin' the craps the way he's used to shootin' them. That's all it is."

Pedro glared up at Curtis, but prudence warned him not to push it. He glanced around and caught his partner's eyes, then glanced down at the money in the pot. His actions were obvious to everybody in the game.

Before the other Mexican could pick his money up out of the dirt, Dan picked up the dice and rolled them out. "Seven, baby," he yelled, as the craps slowly rolled across the dirt.

Before the heavyset Mexican could follow his partner's directions, the dice had rolled out and stopped on a seven. Pedro let out a curse and glared angrily at the dice shooter.

"Seven, and we have a winner," Curtis yelled out, making it clear to the angry Mexicans that it had been a fair roll.

Pedro coughed and cleared his throat. "Yeah, Dannie boy, you really think you're cute, don't you, my man?" His jet-black eyes were flashing dangerously as he tried to control his temper.

Dan, a tall, slim, brown-skinned man in his early twenties, smiled coldly. Though his lips were pulled back in a smile, his dark eyes were bleak and deadly as he watched the Mexican out of the corner of them.

"Hey, Pedro," he called out softly, "what's the deal, man? You say I'm tryin' to be cute. I can't dig that, brother. I'm just tryin' to win some cash money, that's all, my man."

Before Pedro could say anything, his partner punched him in the side with his elbow. "It's okay, dude, you caught me with my pants down on that roll."

Dan smiled at the heavyset Mexican. "That's the way I like to hear people rap, Jay. You win some, you lose some."

Jay Novello, the husky Mexican, ignored Dan as he got up from the crap game. "I think we had better be movin' on, amigo," Jay stated as he reached out and touched the quick-tempered Pedro's arm. "It's nothing, amigo, but a few dollars."

"Hey, brother, wait a minute now. I don't want you to leave with no kind of attitude now, 'cause ain't nobody did nothin' to you," Curtis stated sharply, then added, "'cause if you think you been cheated, run it down to me. I don't run no kind of crooked game, not in my momma's backyard, no way."

Curtis stepped in front of the two men. "Now, if you got some kind of complaint, let's get it off your chest and we can clear up the air right now!"

"We ain't got no complaints, Curtis," Jay stated, "but we done warned this dude six or seven times about shootin' that turn-down shot on us, and he still takes us for tricks."

"Hey, Jay," Curtis replied quietly, "we both saw the shot he used when he rolled seven just now and it wasn't no turn-down shot he used. Before, yes, but you caught the dice, Jay, so now what the fuck is the problem?"

Before Jay could answer, Curtis went on. "Now, if you're hot over losin' your money, I ain't about to replace it, so you're shit out of luck. If you couldn't stand to lose, you shouldn't have started to gamble!"

His words beat at the two men, each one feeling the weight of them as he spoke. Pedro glanced upward at the sky. Jay, on the other hand, glanced down at his shoes, then moved nervously from one foot to the other. He slowly raised his eyes and stared at Curtis.

"Hey, amigo, we ain't fools, you dig? Now, I been beat out of a few dollars," Jay began, speaking with slow deliberation and looking directly into Curtis' eyes. "But the money ain't about nothin', Curtis. What hurts, amigo, is that we thought we were more cooler with you than that."

Jay raised his hand, cutting off whatever Curtis was about to say. "I know without it being said that we been hustled, Curtis, but that ain't about shit. What I'm tryin' to say is, I thought we were tighter than that, but it's okay, my man. Them things happen. Maybe you needed the few dollars that your main man won; who knows, I don't, and I don't give a fuck!"

Curtis frowned but didn't say anything. He listened quietly as the Mexican continued to speak.

"We ain't got no attitude, as you said, Curtis, we just didn't think you'd hustle us." Jay shrugged, looking like an overgrown bulldog at that moment—his pug nose quivering, his black eyes sparkling.

After much shifting about, Pedro managed to get into the conversation. "Yeah, Curtis, we never figured you'd turn on us like that, man. It ain't like it should be. Friends ain't supposed to play on each other, not when they're cool with each other."

Finally Dan got tired of listening to the two complaining Mexicans. "Hey, what kind of shit is this?" he began. "Before you guys get carried away, why don't you dig this sho'nuff shit. It wasn't none of Curtis who ripped you off. It was me, so why the fuck are you wasting your time wearing his eardrums off? I'm the one who beat you out of your money, so if you think you got played on, take it up with me, not him!"

Pedro shifted suddenly and his hand dipped down into his pocket. Jay's words froze him in that position.

"We ain't got no argument with neither one of you," Jay stated. "We got beat, and that's it!"

"Well," Dan drawled, "I just hope your friend happens to feel the way you do about it, Jay, 'cause if he don't, this motherfuckin' sociable little party could turn into somethin' neither one of us wants."

Jay attempted to laugh it off as he gripped Pedro's arm tightly. He could feel the firm muscles tightening and retightening under his fingers. Pedro was quick-tempered and dangerous as any coiled rattlesnake. His temper was unpredictable and no one knew it better than Jay. At the moment, though, Jay didn't want any trouble out of the blacks.

"It ain't about nothin, I said," Jay stated again. This time he gave Pedro a small push and started him toward the side of the house.

Pedro stopped and whirled on his heel. "Hey, Curtis," he said, "I never thought you would sock it to me like that, man."

Curtis folded his arms across his wide chest. "No comprendo, Pedro, my man. I just don't know where you're comin' from. But before we fall out over a little money, I'd rather kick back your money and keep your friendship." But Curtis didn't make any move toward his pocket.

For a second Pedro just stared at him. "I just bet you will," he replied, his cold black eyes never leaving the face of the tall black man he spoke to.

Suddenly Curtis laughed, a cold, chilling sound without any mirth in it. "Hey, my man, I'm going to pull your coat one more time, Pedro, then you can take it any way you want to. This is my mother's pad, man, so I wouldn't start any shit around here, and I sure 'nuff don't want any kind of trouble. So you should be able to understand that."

Seeing that the shit was about to get deep again, Jay didn't waste any time. "Hey, amigo," he said lightly as he took Pedro's arm and turned him back around. This time he didn't try to be gentle. "I said it was all right, Pedro, so forget it, man, you dig?"

"If you say so, Jay," Pedro answered, "but I ain't

about to forget about it."

"Do whatever the fuck you want to do!" Curtis stated sharply.

Dan rubbed his chin as he watched the two Mexicans depart. "You know, Curt, we might have some trouble out of them spics, brother."

Curtis shook his head. "I doubt it. If it was one of the Fernandez brothers, I'd say yes, but our boy Pedro is a blowhard. He's quick-tempered as hell, but he also forgets shit. He won't even think about it this time tomorrow."

"You think he's going to pull his brother's coat that we bumped his head?" Dan inquired.

Again Curtis shrugged his wide shoulders. "It's hard to say, Dan. Right now his pride is hurt, so no tellin'. If he didn't think he was the smartest bastard in the world it would be easy to figure him out, but since he don't think like other people, I don't know. First of all, he might not want his brother to know that he was foolish enough to start shooting craps in my backyard. His pride might not allow him to confess his stupidity to others."

"Well, I hope you're right, Curt, 'cause if you ain't, we goin' have trouble coppin' some good stuff from them Mexes."

"Well, ain't no sense us worryin' 'bout what we can't help, is there, Dan?"

For an answer Dan grinned, then slapped his partner on the back. "Okay, Curt, you know more about these Mexicans than I'll ever be able to find out, so I'll go along with your judgment."

"Good," Curtis replied, "now let's get on into the pad and see what Mom has got together in that big pot she was cookin' in." Curtis didn't wait for an answer as he led the way toward the back door. He pushed the screen door open and stepped in.

The rear porch was crowded with debris. Three large gray ashcans sat near the door that led into the house, while cardboard boxes with various items in them were everywhere. The rear porch was screened in so that people could sit there and enjoy the nights without fear of being eaten to death by insects.

At the sound of the two young men walking on the porch, a woman's voice called out, "Curtis, is that you?"

"Yeah, Ma," he answered quickly as he stopped at the rear door that led into the house and began to wipe his feet off.

"I'm sure glad you boys have finished gambling out there, Curtis," she stated. "You know how much I hate to see you gambling, period, let alone in our yard."

Before he could say anything to an old argument of his mother's, she continued. "One of these days you niggers are going to get yourselves killed over one of them cheap dice games. Hell, I'd be surprised to death if there was over ten dollars in the whole game!"

Both men grinned at each other, then Dan removed the bankroll from his pocket and began to count it. "Shit!" he exclaimed happily, "I believe Jay blowed his whole paycheck." To make sure, he recounted the money in his hand. "Yeah, I won one hundred and fourteen dollars, Curt."

Curtis removed the money from his pocket and quickly counted it. "Good, we got one hundred and fifty dollars between us, Dan. That's more than enough to cop us a good bag of stuff." Curtis held the door open for his friend and partner. "Besides the money, Dan, we got a pot of black-eyed peas waitin' on us inside," he stated as he lifted his nose and smelled deeply. "Yes sirreee, my nose ain't never fucked around and let me down, man. Whenever I tell you what's smokin' in the pot, brother, you can lay money on it I'm right."

The two men entered the kitchen, which was right off the back porch. Curtis' mother, a large, heavyset woman, was standing at the stove. She twisted her head around and smiled at the men. When she opened her mouth, the empty spaces where her teeth had been were visible.

"I just know you done trimmed them Mexicans out of their little bit of money," she stated as the two men settled down in the center of the kitchen at the small table.

"Now, Moms," Curtis began, "we just happened to get lucky today, that's all."

"Shit!" she replied loudly. "If you waited on luck you'd never have a damn thing!" Mrs. Carson said seriously as she waddled away from the stove and made her way across the floor to the white painted cabinet over the kitchen sink. She removed two dishes, carried them back, and set them down in front of the men. Her broad black face broke into a grin as she began to load their plates from a large bowl that had been sitting on the table. She went back to the stove and opened the oven, removed a cornbread pan, cut two large slices and carried them back to put one on each man's plate. Finally, she brought them both large glasses of Kool-Aid and set them on the table.

"Damn!" Dan exclaimed, "I don't know how I'm ever going to get all this food down. Shit, Momma, if I ate at your house every day, I'd weigh over five hundred pounds!"

Mother Carson loved to cook. And next to that, she loved to watch men eat. She prided herself on always having enough, no matter how many friends Curtis or his brother Billy brought home for dinner.

"Where's Billy at?" Curtis inquired as his mother came back to the table, this time carrying some butter in a tray.

Before answering, Mother Carson reached up and wiped the sweat off the red handkerchief she wore wrapped around her head. The bandanna was filthy from long use, while the white apron she wore was almost spotless. Her features were average—for a black housewife over fifty. She was fat to an excess, revealing that she also loved her own cooking just as much as she liked seeing other people eat it.

"I believe your brother is up to the Center playing basketball," she answered in a voice that matched her size.

"Shit, Billy goin' turn into a goddamn basketball one of these days," Curtis stated offhandedly.

"Better for him to spend his time at the Center playing basketball than running the streets like you and Dan. Ain't no good goin' come of it, you can bet your black ass on it, too," she said harshly, not bothering to respect the feeling of her son's guest.

"Now, Momma," Dan began, but he was cut off sharply.

"Don't 'now momma' me," she said harshly. "I know what you two niggers are up to when you're out in them streets, so don't try and shit me." Her voice rose higher as she spoke until she was nearly shouting.

"Momma," Curtis said softly, trying to change the subject, "now we don't need to go into all that crap today, do we?"

She just snorted, then got up from the table and made her way over to the cabinet. When her back was turned, Curtis motioned for Dan to hurry up and eat. He wanted to get away before his mother started to preach.

Their plates were too heavy for the two men to just gulp the food down, so they were still there when she returned carrying another clean plate. She set it down and placed a knife and spoon beside it. The two men could hear what she had heard earlier—someone had entered the front door and was now making the way through the house toward the kitchen.

Suddenly a tall, dark-skinned young boy stood in the doorway. He was slim, yet well put together. His shoulders had the wideness of Curtis', yet he was smaller than his brother. The large shoulders tapered down to a thin waist. From the shorts he wore, you could see the strong legs of the young man. His features were almost identical to those of his older brother. Yet there was a difference. Where Curtis' eyes were cold and hard, Billy had soft eyes—eyes that were not yet ruined by his surroundings.

His mother's face broke into a wide grin at the sight of him, and it could easily be seen that her young son was held in deep respect.

Billy nodded his head, then spoke up. "Naw, Moms, we didn't do nothing but practice today, that's all." He nodded at his brother and Dan, not bothering to speak to either of the men.

"Practice, practice, practice," Curtis said coldly. "Don't you ever get tired of firing that ball at the hoop, Billy?"

"Naw, brother, I don't get any more tired than you do of running up and down the alleys searching for a crap game that you can cheat in!" he drawled, not bothering to conceal the sarcasm in his voice. "Why don't you come on back out for the team, Curt? You used to be the best center in the city, man."

"Big deal," Curtis answered, "and when I was the best center in the city, I couldn't even buy a pair of pants to cover my black ass!"

"Hey, man, everything takes time, Curt, you know that. It was just a matter of time before one of them big colleges gave you a free ride through school. Then after that, shit, man, you could name your own price."

"Yeah, I know. Four fuckin'...."

Before he could go any further, he heard his mother's sharp reprimand. "Okay, now, Curtis, I don't need that kind of language in this house and you know it. It just goes to show what you pick up in the street. You don't respect nobody anymore!"

"I'm sorry, Moms," Curtis began, trying to apologize. It just slipped out, that's all. You know I didn't mean no disrespect by it."

"Yeah, Curtis, I know you didn't," she answered slowly, "but that's just what I'm talking about. Those streets teach you them things."

Dan finished his plate of food and pushed it to the middle of the table. Mrs. Carson glanced out of the corner of her eyes to see if he had finished everything. It was wiped clean, so she didn't make any comment.

Curtis followed his friend's action, only his plate wasn't as clean. His mother gave him a cold stare but again didn't make any comment. As the two men got up from the table, she pushed back the seat she had taken and followed them toward the door.

"Curtis," she began as they walked slowly toward the door that led out of the kitchen and into the hallway to the living room, "if you see your sister anywhere, you tell her to get her butt home. It's way past time for her to be home from summer school. Goodness, I don't know which one of you will put me in my grave first, you or Rita!"

As the men walked briskly through the hallway, Curtis didn't bother to answer. He had heard this statement all his life. It seemed as if he had been putting his mother in her grave ever since he was a little boy. But even though he didn't mention it to his mother, he would make sure Rita got her ass home if he saw her on the streets. He hated to see the crowd she ran with. All the girls were easy, and wild as hell.

The freshly painted hallway was long. The three bedrooms in the house were set off from the hallway. Two were on one side, while the other bedroom with the toilet next to it was on the other side. When the men reached the living room, their steps were silenced by the thick carpet. It wasn't wall-to-wall carpeting but the accumulation of three old rugs piled on top of each other, which gave that effect. The top rug was reddish and checkered, matching the black couch and chair that took up most of the room. The living room contained a dining room set that no elderly woman would do without in the early sixties. It included a matching china cabinet where the good dishes were kept on display.

Mother Carson followed the two men right to the front door. She even held it open as they went out. "Now remember, Curtis, send your sister home if you see her, hear?"

Curtis glanced irritably at his mother; then the feeling died as he saw the worried look in her face. She didn't really mean any harm, but she did get on his nerves with her constant nagging about the so-called "dangers of the streets."

"Don't worry, Moms," Curtis replied, then leaned over and kissed her on the cheek. It was something he hadn't done for quite a few years, and he could see the surprise come into her eyes as he removed his arms from around her neck and stepped back. "Just do like I said, Momma, and don't worry. If you want, I'll go out of my way and find her and see to it that she gets her ass home."

As a nod of appreciation came from her, he grinned and caught up with Dan. "Don't worry, Mrs. Carson," Dan called out, "I'll look after both of them for you!" He laughed loudly and pounded Curtis on the back. Mrs. Carson stood in the doorway and watched the two men make their way down the street. She knew she shouldn't worry, but Curtis reminded her too much of her husband, and it was all too clear in her mind how he had died. As long as she lived, she would always believe the streets had killed her husband, and every night she prayed to the Lord that the streets wouldn't likewise be the death of her older son.

2

DAN AND CURTIS ONLY had to walk three blocks before they were up on the set. The black-topped New Mexico street where they hung out consisted of two poolrooms and four bars, two bars on each side of the street. Soldiers staggered from one bar to the next on weekends as they sought the few good-looking whores who worked the bars and the street corner.

Their first stop was a poolroom, where Curtis inquired about the whereabouts of Fat George, an old Mexican who was the largest dope dealer on their side of town. Not seeing Fat George's new Cadillac, Curtis knew it would take a while before George showed up. Since the man hadn't given Curtis any phone number when they had talked a few days ago, all he could do was wait and hope that the Mexican would show up some time that evening.

"What do you think?" Dan inquired, as the two men came out of the first poolroom and walked slowly towards the next one.

"What do I think about what?" Curtis asked vacantly, letting his thoughts wander.

"About George, that's what. Do you think he's going to show up or what?" Dan asked, not letting the subject drop.

His mind still wandering, Curtis gave a shrug; then he stopped suddenly in the street. "I'll bet that silly little bitch is hanging out over at the Do-Drop-Inn!"

"Maybe," Dan replied. "Ain't but one way to find out for sure, though."

Both men set off walking down the street. The Do-Drop-Inn was a restaurant and bar, but it didn't sell whiskey, only beer and wine, the specialty being a large pitcher of draft beer that was the favorite of most of the customers.

The age restriction was supposed to be eighteen and up, but the owner, Joe, allowed the young girls in the neighborhood to come in. The boys were another case. If a dude couldn't show proof that he was eighteen he wouldn't be allowed inside the place. Some boys who were really old enough to get in still had trouble if they didn't have their identification on them when Joe asked for it.

The bar was located in the middle of the block, across the street from one of the poolrooms. The first thing that reached the two men as they entered the club was the loud sound of the jukebox. Curtis had to blink his eyes before they became accustomed to the darkness of the place. The restaurant part of the club was in the front. Tables were set up in the middle of the floor, while neat rows of booths were along the wall. To reach the club part, where the drinking and dancing went on, a customer had to walk to the rear of the club and enter through the back door. It was just one step down and then you were in the club. Here too booths lined the wall, while small tables filled the center of the club.

There was no actual bar, only a large dance area in the middle of the floor. When a customer ordered a pitcher of beer, the waitress had to walk over to the window that opened into the kitchen. There was a woman standing there whose only job was taking the orders from the three waitresses, who stayed busy delivering the drinks to the tables.

Now as Curtis glanced around the club, he could see the place was crowded with soldiers from the near-by base. They came in at all hours of the day to dance and try and make it with the young girls who sometimes skipped school so that they could hang out at the Do-Drop-Inn.

"Over here," Dan said, and pointed at a booth in the rear of the club. As Curtis followed Dan's direction he saw a group of young girls and two soldiers packed together in the booth. In the dimness of the club, it was hard to make them out. But as Curtis stared, he heard the high laughter of one of the girls and he knew then that he had found Rita. There was no mistaking her loud laughter. No one laughed the same way she did.

Curtis led the way toward the rear of the club. As they neared the booth, Rita saw her brother coming and began to get up from the table. Ordinarily Curtis didn't interfere with what she did, so she was surprised to see him approaching her.

The owner of the club, Joe, watched from his private table next to the dance floor. He knew Curtis by sight, and he knew Curtis' sister was underage. The last thing he wanted was any kind of trouble out of some angry brother—not over any young girl. It was too easy for him to lose his license, even though he paid off the police regularly.

Before Rita and Curtis met, Joe was up and moving his huge bulk toward them. "Your momma is worried about you, Rita, so you better get on home and see what she wants."

"Shit!" Rita exploded, revealing at once that she had had too much beer to drink. "I ain't no child, Curt, so I don't know why the hell you're going out of your way to run me down."

At first, Curtis was surprised by her reply, then anger welled up inside of him. "Hey, Sis, this is Curt, your big brother, not one of these phony-ass niggers you mess around with down here, so don't give me any of your shit. I don't want to hear it!"

"Well," she said, pouting, "I ain't in no hurry to go home, so you just run along and take care of whatever business you got to take care of!"

Joe stared at the tall, brown-skinned girl with the short mini-skirt. He had wished many a time that he could've gotten into her drawers. Big legs and large tits, though her facial features were more mannish than he would have liked. She had a short natural hairstyle that made her resemble a man even more, while her nose was short and blunt. Her eyes were the same as her brother's, jet black with heavy eyebrows. She had the same height that the men in her family had, standing almost six feet tall without shoes. And while wearing the latest style, the huge heels, she towered over six feet. Still, one could see she was still young and had some more growing to do. When she smiled, she revealed evenly spaced white teeth. But there was something cruel about her. It could be seen in her face—a cattish look. Yet many men would still think she was very lovely.

Now as she spoke, there was nothing lovely about her. Her lips were formed into a sneer. "I ain't in no hurry, Curt, to go home and hear no fuckin' preaching," she said, putting her hands on her hips.

Before Joe could interfere, Curtis' hand came up in a blur and he slapped her viciously across the face. One of the soldiers jumped up from the table where he had been watching the two.

"You just hold onto that fuckin' seat," Joe warned. "Curtis, I don't need that kind of shit in here, so you get your sister on out, but no more slaps, okay?"

Curtis stared coldly at the fat black man. At first he wanted to give Joe a hard time but quickly realized that the owner of the club was right.

The slap had brought Rita to her senses. She knew she had pushed her brother too far and she had no intention of pushing him any further. He must have been mad about something else, she reflected, because he rarely put his hands on her. It had been years since he had last slapped her.

"Damn, Curt," she moaned softly, "you didn't have to do that."

"I just don't want to hear any of your smart lip, Rita," he said, beckoning toward the door. "Now, let's get the hell out of here."

Dan glared at the soldier who still wanted to come to the girl's rescue, not so much to really help her but because she had drunk up so much of his beer and he had hoped to get her into the nearest motel. Now she was being led away by her brother, so the money he had spent on her was all wasted.

Dan stepped back and let Rita walk past him. He couldn't help but admire the large ass she had. With the miniskirt riding high on her hips, he got a good look at what he liked to see. If she ever bent over, he reflected, she'd have to show her natural ass. The skirt was so short that just the slightest bend in her back would reveal the color of the drawers that she wore.

No one spoke until they were on the sidewalk in front of the Do-Drop-Inn. It had been Curtis' plan to walk her home, but as they reached the street, the first thing he saw was Fat George pulling up in his late-model Cadillac. Dan spotted him at the same time.

"Looks like we're running in luck," Dan stated.

"Rita," Curtis began, "I want you to take your ass

on home now. I ain't going to follow you, but I mean for you to go there, you dig?" He waited a second, then added, "I'll be home in about fifteen minutes, so I want to see you when I get there. Now, you can act cute if you want to and not go home, but whenever I find you, I'm going to kick the living shit out of you! You understand where I'm coming from?"

"Naw," she answered harshly, "I don't know where you're coming from, but I'll do what you say." She hesitated for a second, then added, "Curt, I don't know what's buggin' you, bro, but I don't dig this shit of yours coming down on me like I'm your whore or something."

"Well, that's too damn bad," he replied, "but you ain't but sixteen, so if you give me any trouble I'll personally see to it that Joe don't let you in his joint no more."

The threat of being kept out of Joe's was enough to make her change her ways quickly. Joe's was the only place in town for young girls to really have fun. Other than that, she would have to go over to one of her girlfriends' houses to dance, and that was really boring. Their parents would be watching, and none of them allowed their young daughters to bring any soldiers home. It was the same with her mother. She wouldn't allow a soldier in the house. She thought the soldiers would try to take advantage of her daughter.

If there was one thing Rita didn't want, it was her brother telling her mother that she was with some soldiers. She might have to stay home for a week or two before she would be allowed back out on the streets.

"Aw, Curt," she began, pleading openly, "you and me ain't never had no misunderstanding that we couldn't rap about, bro. I'm sorry if I said anything out of the way back there, but I been drinkin' a little too much beer, that's all. I got myself together now, so ain't we still cool with each other?" She flashed him her most pleasing smile, showing the well-kept teeth that she was so proud of.

Curtis had to smile in return. "Don't worry, Rita, I ain't goin' to do no tattletelling this time, just as long as you do like I said and take your fat ass home."

Rita started walking in the direction of their house, waving back over her shoulder at her brother. "Bring me a pop when you come home," she called back as she continued on her way.

Trying not to be observed, Dan watched the young girl walk away. Her legs were bowed just enough to give her that real sexual look as she walked. Wide-legged, her young hips swayed smoothly with each long step she took.

"She's too young for you, Dan," Curtis stated as he caught the look on his partner's face.

"Hey, my man, you don't think I'd have any thoughts in that direction, would you? Shit, Curt, I look at Rita as if she's my young sister or something, man."

"Yeah, I just bet you do," Curt replied slowly. "From the way you were digging her ass, I'd hate to see what you would do to your own sister!"

"Aw, man," Dan said, guilt all over his face, "I'm sorry you think that way."

"Forget it," Curtis replied as he began to lead the way toward the parked car. As they neared the Ford, a large, heavyset Mexican came out of the bar and stopped on the sidewalk. He spoke jokingly with the people lounging in front of the club.

"What it is," Curtis stated as they neared the man. "I hear you're gettin' all the money in town, George."

Fat George turned and smiled in his direction. "What's happenin', Curtis? Who you and Dan been rippin' off lately?" George asked him as they came up on the sidewalk.

Both men grinned at the so-called "big man" as they neared him. "How about takin' us over on Hill Street? We got somethin' to pick up you might like," Curtis asked as they stopped in front of George.

Fat George caught on at once. "Hey, man, you know I ain't no taxi, but this time I'll do it for you two guys, 'cause you're all right with me." George spoke loudly for the benefit of the idle loafers in front of the bar.

Anything that was said would be repeated a hundred times after the men left. The loafers didn't have anything else to do but meddle in other people's business. Their lives were wasted. Most of them would never get any farther than Main Street in New Mexico. They would spend their whole lives in useless loafing in front of one bar or another. Then sometimes you'd find them piled inside someone's car, drinking and laughing.

The door on the passenger side of the car was locked, so Curtis and Dan had to stand on the sidewalk and wait until George got in and unlocked the door. Before they pulled off, one of the loafers came away from the storefront and walked in front of the car. He came around to the driver's side. George let his window down quickly, removing the bored expression that flashed across it.

"Yeah, Hip Daddy," George said to the small black man who approached the car, "what can I do for you?"

"Hey, George, I couldn't help but overhear what ya said, so how about dropping me off up near Ninth Street. You're going right past there, you know, if you're takin' Curt and Dan up to Hill Street."

"Yeah, man, I can dig what you're sayin', but if you heard what I said, you must not have heard the part I said about I ain't no fuckin' taxi, you dig? I'm doing Curtis a favor 'cause I want him to do somethin' for me, but I ain't got no time to drop you off on Ninth Street, Hip Daddy," George stated, then hit the button and ran his window back up before the man could say anything else.

George spoke to the two men inside the car. "I can't get over the nerve of some of these niggers. I mean, look at that shit Hip Daddy is wearing. Them pants he got on are filthy. Now, common sense should tell him that I don't want him in my ride with all that grease on his clothes. Shit, I'd never get it out of this white upholstery I got. But if I was to tell him the truth, his feelings would be hurt, while I'd be in trouble if I was stupid enough to let him in my ride."

Curtis had to agree with him. One look at the nasty overalls that Hip Daddy wore was enough to make

George's point. The man looked as if he had been working on some cars in a garage somewhere. Dirt and oil were everywhere on the man's pants. But it hadn't stopped him from asking for a ride. In fact, Curtis reflected as he thought about it, he doubted if the thought had even entered Hip Daddy's mind.

"Now, what can I do for you guys?" George inquired as he drove away from the curb.

Curtis waited until he had turned a corner before asking. "You know what I asked you about last week, don't you, George?"

"Yeah, I just forget how much it was. I can handle it, you dig, that ain't no problem. Now, what was it you wanted? Was it raw stuff or mixed dope? Which one? It don't make no difference to me which one you want."

"We got a bill fifty," Dan said quickly, causing Curtis to flinch angrily.

George let out a short laugh. "Hey, amigo, don't worry about it. Old George ain't goin' give you no screwing. You ain't got to worry. Now, let's get down to facts. You guys are just gettin' started, right?"

He waited until Curtis had nodded his head in agreement, then continued. "Okay then, dig this. Curt, you ain't got no milk sugar yet, have you?" Again he waited for the head shake. "Okay, then, now listen while I pull your coat to something. If you ain't got the right bankroll, it's goin' set you back tryin' to buy milk sugar to cut your dope with." George hesitated briefly, letting his words sink in. "Now, I don't give a shit what you buy, Curt, but since you're just gettin' started, I can help you out."

"Okay, George, I know we don't know that much about this jive, but we ain't above listenin' to somebody who can pull our coats to the real deal."

George let out a short laugh. "Okay, good, we got a understandin', that's good. I like you, Curt, that ain't no bullshit. If I didn't, I wouldn't waste my time. Now, dig this. It would be better if you bought mixed dope from me this time. While you're selling it, you can use some of the money you make and purchase the milk sugar you'll be needin' when your money is right and you buy raw dope."

"How much is the mix goin' cost us?" Dan inquired seriously.

"Too much!" George replied quickly. "Unless you've got more than one fifty. If that's all the cash you've got, you're going to need it to get started. Or," he continued with a large smile, "you had better go and find another Fernandez brother and bust him."

"Well, I'll be damned," Dan cursed quietly. "It don't take long for shit to spread, does it?"

"Aw hell, Dan," Curt said, "don't you know Mexicans are tight as hell? Don't nothin' happen to one that the rest of them don't find out about."

Again George let out his phony laugh. "That's right, especially when one gets played on by one of you brothers, the message spreads quickly."

"Played on, hell; the bastard just lost his money, that's all," Dan alibied quickly.

"Yeah, man," George replied, drawing the last word out, "I know just what you mean."

"Fuck that shit!" Curtis stated sharply. "It ain't no skin off your ass no way, is it, George?"

George shook his head quickly. "Naw," he answered, the lie revealed in every line in his face. "Why the shit should I care what some dumb-ass spic goes and does? As long as it wasn't my money, I could care less."

Both the black men knew at once that the man was lying to them. Curtis asked the question that was on both of their minds. "I hope that shit don't cause us to fall out over the dope you sell me, George. I mean, I dig you and all that shit, but my money comes too damn hard for me to get some bunk for it."

"Hey, amigo, this is George you're talkin' to. Like I said, whatever some other cat goes and does don't mean shit to me, and if it did, I wouldn't let it come before me and my business, Curtis."

Curtis nodded his head in agreement. "I'm hoping you see it thataway, George, because if we work it right, there will be plenty of green stuff in it for both of us."

"Yeah, man," Dan said, speaking his little bit. "It ain't about nothin', that crap game, 'cause it was me that beat them dudes out of their bread anyway, not Curt."

It was obvious that George was irritated by Dan's words. "Listen, man," he began, "me and Curt are going to do the business, you dig? I don't know nothing about you, so if you don't mind, you stay out of it. I know you were the one who rolled the dice, as well as I know that if Curtis hadn't been there, they would have took their money back."

The man's words stung. Dan winced under them, but before he could speak, Curtis spoke up because he knew that Dan's pride had been hurt.

"We should completely forget about the crap game, George. It was unavoidable, and I regret that it happened."

"Well, I don't," Dan yelled, continuing to keep the subject open. "If the studs were out of their league playin', that was their problem, not mine."

"Hey, man," George said softly, "the studs thought it was just a friendly game. They didn't know Curtis was in on the hustle. I mean, shootin' craps in Curtis' backyard has always been a thing we have gone in for. After today, who knows, but I can promise you this, you won't ever pick up any more easy money like that!"

"Shit!" Curtis cursed, "you guys just ain't going to let it drop, are you?" He took out his cigarettes and quickly lit one. "If you want me to, George, I'll make the guy's money right. I just want an end to it."

George shrugged his fat shoulders. "Forget it, man. It's over and done. Pedro needed a lesson. Now maybe he'll believe he ain't the smartest guy in the world."

"You can say that again," Dan stated, then laughed sardonically.

For some reason, Dan seemed to get on George's nerves. Every time he spoke, the fat man seemed to get aroused. "You know, Curt, it don't take all of us to take care of this business, so why don't we drop your friend off somewhere and you can pick him back up when you get back over here."

"No bet, man. My money ain't going out of my sight," Dan said angrily.

"Hold it," Curtis said quickly. "You realize what you're sayin', Dan?" His temper rose. "George, stop at the corner and let Dan out. My mother stays about five blocks from here. If you want to, you can walk over there and wait until I get back with the stuff. If not, well, it's your decision."

Before Curtis was finished speaking, George had pulled to the curb and parked. Dan glared angrily at the fat man. "Hey, Curt, let me talk to you privately for a second, huh?"

"Hey, man, I ain't got all day. Either we take care of the business or pass it up to another fuckin' time," George stated.

Curtis shook his head. "It ain't necessary for all that shit, Dan. I know what's got to be done, so why go to all this bullshit." Curtis was trying to make his partner cool down.

"Fuck that shit, Curt," Dan said hotly. "This fat motherfucker think he's playin' games with us, but it ain't about nothin', Curt. We can cop some jive anyplace. We ain't got to deal with this chili-bean-eatin' motherfucker!"

"Hey, man, I ain't got all them names," George said slowly, his fat cheeks turning red.

"You'll be all them names and any more I want to call you, fat-ass motherfucker," Dan yelled as he opened the car door.

"Dan, Dan," Curtis yelled at his friend, "cool down

a minute, man. This shit ain't about nothing. It ain't no problem for you to wait until I get back from coppin', man."

"I ain't waitin' nowhere, Curt. We began together and we'll finish together, if we're going to be real partners."

The two men glared at each other. Then Curtis broke the short silence. "Well, it don't make sense coppin' nowhere else, Dan. George got the best jive in the city, so it ain't good business to go elsewhere."

"The fat motherfucker don't want to do no business with me, Curt, 'cause I trimmed them other bean-eatin' motherfuckin' spics, man. So I ain't about to kiss his ass to get along with him," Dan stated loudly.

"Ain't nobody asked you to do nothin', Dan. All you got to do is give me your bread and wait until I get back, that's all."

Dan shook his head stubbornly. "Like I said before, Curt, I ain't about to let my money get out of my sight. Now, if he wants to do business with us, he'll do it with both of us, like he started out to do. Other than that, he can kiss my black ass!"

Dan slammed the car door and glared back through the open window. "It ain't nothing about you, Curt; it's just that I don't like the way this fat motherfucker came down on us. Now, if you want to still go through with it yourself, that's up to you."

"Yeah, man," Curtis answered softly, "I ain't changed my mind. George still got the best dope in town, and I want some of it."

With slow deliberation, Dan spit on the hood of the

car, then slowly extracted the bankroll from his pocket. His cold black eyes never left the face of the angry
Mexican. He counted out the money, then pushed sev-
enty-five dollars back through the window.

"Here's your share of the money for trimming them
two trick-ass Mexicans, Curt. If you ever get some
more dumb-ass wetbacks over your way, give me a
ring and I'll be glad to come over and relieve them
stupid motherfuckers from their bankroll!" As soon as
he finished speaking, he again spit on top of the car's
hood, making sure George saw him do it.

George pulled away from the curb quickly, his
cheeks a flaming red. He couldn't hide his anger, nor
could he hide the fear that had gripped him. For a
brief minute, he hadn't known which way the angry
Negro would go. Violence was one thing he wanted
no part of, not when he might be on the receiving end
of it.

"That crazy sonofabitch," George said as he drove
swiftly through the traffic. "I'll fix his fuckin' ass one
of these days, Curt, I promise you that!"

Both men fell silent, each thinking his own bitter
thoughts. Curt realized that now his money wasn't
anywhere near right. How could he cop with only half
the price of a bag? He came right to the point.

"Well, ain't no reason for me to beat around the
bush, George," he began. "You went and blew it for
me. I needed Dan's share of the money to make my
bankroll right. When you went out of your way to
arouse him, you blew it for me!"

Fat George shrugged his shoulders, then lit a cigar.

The smell of the brown cigar filled the car. "Don't worry about it, Curt. Like I said, I always have liked you, so we can make it up whenever you cop again." He waited for a second, then added, "How does that sound to you, huh?"

For the first time since Dan got out of the car, Curtis sat back and relaxed. Things might work out even better now. Without a partner there would be more money for him and less of a problem.

"Yeah, George," he replied, smiling briefly, "things just might work out all right after all."

3

IT TOOK ONLY A COUPLE of weeks for the man with the four-to-one pop to gain a reputation. The junkies down on Main Street began dropping by Curtis' pad day and night, seeking the fine white powder that mixed a little more to their liking than the other stuff in town.

Curtis was making the bread, and Fat George couldn't have been more pleased with the arrangement. He was supplying Curtis, giving him any quantity that he needed, leaving himself open for more leisure time and a little less hassle. The one goal that George sought was to get himself away from the addicts, far enough away so that their unpredictable

behavior would never affect him. Pushing his stuff
through Curtis was the man's way of handling it.

For both men, the situation seemed to have a future.
They could each look ahead, count their money, and
plan on making gains.

After two months of hustling the streets, Curtis
decided it was time to settle into a more reputable
scene. His lifestyle was suspect. He knew that he
could be spotted easily and that his movements left
little doubt as to what he did for a living. With the
amount of money he was making and the kinds of
dudes he was selling to, he decided that it was high
time to get himself into a cozy little apartment—at
least for the time being.

It was a hot, muggy afternoon. Curtis cruised
around in his old Buick for three hours, following up
ads for apartments that he had seen in the local news-
paper. He knew what he was looking for, but none of
the places he had seen so far fit the bill.

Curtis wanted a place where there were lots of people—kids and their mothers, fathers coming home
from work, and a couple of times a week bringing a
few of the boys with them for beer. He wanted action
around him, bodies moving all the time. That kind of
a place would make his comings and goings, plus the
ceaseless flow of junkies that would be visiting him,
much less obvious. Living alone in a secluded little
place raised the suspicions of the nosy neighbors who
tended to live in those kinds of places. For the time
being, anyway, Curtis wanted to lose himself in a
crowd.

The end of the day was approaching fast, and Curtis knew he didn't have much time left. He had people coming at eight o'clock that night, meeting him in the backyard of his mother's place. The sun was low in the western sky, and the mugginess of the day had all but worn him out.

There was one last apartment house on his list, a place located just three blocks off of Main Street. Curtis figured that the location was good because most of the junkies he dealt with didn't have rides, and a place within walking distance would increase his business. He drove over to the Paradise Apartments and stopped in front.

The building was old and gray, with two dilapidated palm trees in front. Curtis leaned out his window and peered through the iron gates into the courtyard. A small pool was filled with children, and he could see three or four motherly types sitting around, smoking cigarettes and talking. The scene looked right.

The manager was an old black woman with two teeth missing in front. She talked with a lisp, and shook the stairway when she led Curtis up to the second-floor apartment.

"A young dude like yourself..., this is a good place." She smiled obscenely up at him, holding the door open.

The apartment was a one-bedroom, furnished in deep green and generally clean. The kitchen window looked out onto the street, and Curtis considered that a good point. Anybody coming toward the building from Main Street would have to make the turn at the end of the street. They would be visible from his kitchen.

"How much, ma'am?" Curtis asked, giving the lady his best college grin.

"Hunnerd an' ten...."

Curtis reached into his pocket, aware of the lady's careful gaze. He pulled out three hundred-dollar bills and a fifty.

"Here," he said, handing her the three-fifty. "Take it for the next three months. I don't want to be hassled with no rent for that amount of time. You dig?"

"Yessir!" the old woman replied, holding the money and wavering between giving him change or trying to rip him off for the extra twenty.

Curtis showed her to the front door, took the door key from her, and led her out onto the balcony. "And listen, ma'am, you just take that extra twenty in there and buy yourself something nice. Okay?"

The old woman was speechless. She looked up at Curtis and smiled, clutching the money in her hands. As Curtis watched her walk unsteadily across the balcony toward the stairway, he knew that there would be no problem from her——ever.

From that moment on, Curtis worked out of his new pad. It was easy going. The junkies liked it there and felt safe. The people who lived around him never knew what was coming down. They were all too busy with their own lives to worry about the lean, dark dude who had moved in upstairs. It was a good scene, and was to get even better.

Curtis saw Shirley the second day. He was standing out on the balcony, having just made a good three hundred off of one dude who was about to take a little journey to L.A. and needed some warmth for his bus ride. Curtis was feeling good, sipping a beer and watching the women and their children down by the pool.

Shirley was sitting with her three children on the patio. She was light-skinned, Mexican, with a head of the finest, blackest hair he had ever seen. Most of the other women around the pool were fat and showed signs of too many children. But not Shirley. Her bikini was small enough to reveal her long, lean legs and her rich, full thighs. Her stomach was flat, and her breasts pushed evenly against her tiny bra. Curtis watched her for the better part of an hour as she languished beneath the hot New Mexico sun.

Curtis' attention was diverted by a tall black dude who ambled into the courtyard. He watched as the man walked across the patio below directly toward Shirley. The beautiful woman said something to one of the other ladies, then got up and walked back toward her first-floor apartment. The black dude followed her, making his way along the opposite side of the pool. Curtis watched as he disappeared into her apartment.

He had never spoken with the girl, but Curtis was fuming. He couldn't understand the anger he felt, or the disappointment. It seemed impossible that he would even have a chance with such a beautiful woman, but nevertheless the rage was still there.

When the man appeared after only a couple of minutes, Curtis was relieved. At least the chick wasn't a working whore. He had seen so many housewives take on afternoon jobs to keep the spending money coming in that he automatically assumed that that was what this woman was doing. But two minutes wasn't even long enough time for them to get mellow.

The black man walked across the patio and left the apartment building. Shirley came out of her apartment a moment later. While she walked back toward her kids, she looked up at Curtis and smiled. It was the kind of look that made Curtis uncomfortable, because it revealed a knowledge in her.

The next day, Curtis watched from his living room window. He saw his old friend and one-time partner, Dan, walk into the courtyard and go to Shirley's apartment. Dan emerged a second later, strutting happily back toward the entrance.

"Dan, my man. What it is?" Curtis shouted down.

Dan stopped in his tracks and looked up at the figure of Curtis. "Hey! Curtis, baby. Wha's happenin'?"

"Come on up, Dan. Show you my pad.... I just moved in here!"

Dan looked around for a moment. He was always suspicious. When he had decided that there was nothing going on, he climbed the steps to the second story, ambled up to Curtis, and gave him a slap.

"Long time, man," Dan said, smiling.

"Yeah, baby. Come on inside and have a beer. I got some things I got to know."

Dan looked at his old friend curiously, then followed Curtis into the apartment. There was still the tension of that night with Fat George between them, and Dan was highly aware of his own feelings. He was also badly in need of a fix. But that would have to wait because Dan wasn't about to admit to Curtis that he was mainlining. A few snorts had been his scene when they had been together ripping the Fernandez brothers off for a few nickels and dimes. But that had been the limit. Curtis was one of those dudes you didn't admit to using in front of, because Curtis didn't use himself. And Dan knew that Curtis would never consider taking him on as a partner if he found out that Dan was on the needle.

Dan still had hopes of getting in on the scoring end, but at the same time, he knew that his chances for making it in that kind of scene were evaporating as fast as he could puncture his veins with the needle. Time was definitely not on his side. It hadn't been since the night he had confronted Fat George.

Curtis came out of the kitchen with two cans of beer. He tossed one to Dan, then sat down in the armchair, resting his feet on the coffee table.

"How you been, Dan?"

"Groovy, Curtis. Nothin' happenin' with me that ain't fine...." Dan took a long swig of his beer.

"Still snortin' the powder?"

Dan lowered his can and stared down at the floor. "Ain't nothin' about nothin' doin' that shit, Curtis. You know that as well as me."

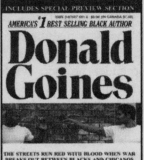